FOOLS FOR

Love

FOOLS FOR Love

KAREN BALL

JENNIFER BROOKS

ANNIE JONES

PALISADES

FOOLS FOR LOVE
published by Palisades
a division of Multnomah Publishers, Inc.

"Jericho's Walls" © 1998 by Karen Ball
"Cat in the Piano" © 1998 by Jennifer Brooks
"Fool Me Twice" © 1998 by Annie Jones

International Standard Book Number: 1-57673-235-5

Cover illustration by Paul Bachem
Cover design by Brenda McGee

Printed in the United States of America

Scripture quotations are from:
The Holy Bible, New International Version (NIV) © 1973, 1984 by International
Bible Society, used by permission of Zondervan Publishing House
and
Holy Bible, New Living Translation (NLT) © 1996.
Used by permission of Tyndale House Publishers, Inc.

For information:
MULTNOMAH PUBLISHERS, INC.
POST OFFICE BOX 1720
SISTERS, OREGON 97759

Library of Congress Cataloging-in-Publication Data
Ball, Karen, 1957–
    Fools for love/by Karen Ball, Jennifer Brooks, Annie Jones
        p. cm.
    ISBN (invalid) 1-57673-232-5 (paper)
    1. Love stories, American. I. Brooks, Jennifer. II. Jones,
Annie, 1957– III. Title.
PS648.L6B35 1998
813'.540803543-dc21   97-43804
                                                          CIP

98 99 00 01 02 03 — 10 9 8 7 6 5 4 3 2 1

JERICHO'S WALLS

KAREN BALL

To Mom and Dad.
Your laughter and love have filled my life and my heart.

"You can make many plans, but the Lord's purpose will prevail."
PROVERBS 19:21

PROLOGUE

Mr. Hawk, you just received a rather odd letter by special delivery. I know I usually open your mail for you, but this is marked personal. And, well, frankly I'm not sure what to do with it."

Brendan Hawk, computer genius extraordinaire, looked up from his computer screen and considered his secretary's hesitant words.

"Where's the letter?"

She held it out to him, and he broke into a grin. The envelope was made of cut and taped old newspapers, and his name and address were written in black crayon across the front.

Gramps. It had to be.

He held out his hand. "I'll take it, Lisa."

His secretary regarded him curiously, then handed it over. As she left the office, Brendan settled back in his chair and reached for his letter opener. "Hawk Computer Consultation" was blazoned across the handle of the stylish, acrylic device. He smiled in satisfaction. That was one promotional item that had worked like a charm. He'd had a host of inquiries as a result of sending them out.

Slitting the top of the letter, he pulled the note free and opened it. A bark of laughter escaped him. The message was pure Gramps: short, concise, and definite: "Come see me. Now." Brendan reached forward to press the intercom button.

"Yes, sir?" came Lisa's usual quick response.

"Lisa, cancel my meetings for today," he said, still smiling. "It appears I have an appointment."

"Um, Doctor Hawk, a note just came for you."

Kylie Hawk looked up from the golden retriever whose teeth she was inspecting.

"Shelley, I'm a bit busy here. Can it wait?"

The young receptionist shrugged. "I suppose, but it came by special delivery, so I thought it might be important."

Kylie sighed and patted the dog on the head. "Okay," she said, holding out her hand. "Let's take a look."

"What's up?"

Kylie glanced over her shoulder to find Alan, one of the other vets, peeking over her shoulder at the envelope she held. She shook her head. "I'm not sure." She looked at the envelope, then grinned. It was made of newspaper and addressed in black crayon.

"Gramps."

"He's in the envelope?" Alan teased.

Kylie laughed. "No, but I'm willing to bet he sent it." She grinned. "It's just the kind of thing he'd do."

Alan took in the handmade envelope and arched his brows. "What is he? Senile?"

Kylie laughed out loud at that. "Not at all. He's just…eccentric."

"That happens when people age sometimes."

"Yeah, well, Gramps was born that way," she returned with a grin. "He's amazing. My mom tells stories about when she was a kid. She thought everyone's parents were like hers."

"Come on, they couldn't have been that unique."

"Oh, yes they could." Kylie giggled. "It wasn't until Mom

was in grade school that she realized it wasn't exactly the norm to have your father rise before the sun every day, brew a strong pot of coffee, and then go climb a ladder up to the roof. There he'd sit, drinking the coffee from a thermos and reading the early morning edition of the paper."

Alan's expression was priceless. "You're kidding."

She shook her head. "Nope. He sat up there every day. According to Mom, he said it was the best place in town to watch the day come to life."

"Was your grandmother weird, too?"

Kylie smiled warmly as the image of her grandmother came to mind. "Grams's distinction was—and is, for that matter—that she always wore these beautiful, brightly colored straw hats and colorful gauzy dresses that swooshed when she floated by. Oh yes, and that she quoted Shakespeare or Longfellow or Hawthorne or a dozen other classical writers at the slightest provocation." Kylie shrugged. "It was just her way of carrying on a conversation."

Alan laughed. "They sound like a hoot."

"They are that," Kylie replied, pulling the note from the envelope and reading it. "Hey, Alan, do me a favor?"

"Anytime."

"Finish checking the golden's teeth for me?"

"Sure," Alan said, watching curiously as she slipped off her white vet's smock. "You going someplace? I thought you were here 'til six."

Kylie gave him a rueful shrug. "I thought I was, too. But something's come up. Fortunately Madison there was my last scheduled appointment today, so it shouldn't be a problem." She hung her smock in the closet and grabbed her jacket and purse.

"What's so important?" Alan asked, obviously surprised.

Kylie couldn't blame him. She was usually the last one to leave the animal clinic.

"I haven't a clue," she said with a wave. "But I can hardly wait to find out."

Brendan pulled into the driveway of his grandparents' home just in time to see his sister, Kylie, getting out of her car.

"Yo, sister mine," he said as he pushed open the car door and got out. "So it looks like this is a regular family confab, eh?"

"Any idea what's up?" Kylie asked, falling into step beside him as they walked up the cobblestone path to the front door.

Brendan shrugged. "I can only think of one thing."

She sighed. "Mom?"

"Mom," he confirmed with a nod.

The doorbell chimed, and Kylie grinned. "Okay, which tune is it this time?"

Brendan rang it again, listening carefully. "It's one of those golden oldies.… Oh yeah!" And he swept Kylie into his arms for an impromptu dance as he sang, "Let me call you *sweet*-heart—"

"I forgot your naaame," Kylie supplied in perfect tune.

"That's not how the song goes, dear, and you know it."

The siblings stopped their whirling and turned to grin at their grandfather, who was standing in the open doorway. "Come on in, you two," he said, stepping aside. "Grams put milk and cookies on the table for us before she went shopping."

"Fresh cookies?" Brendan said eagerly, muscling Kylie out of the way.

"Hey, bozo! Where's your manners?"

"With your brains," he retorted over his shoulder, "on leave."

In short order, they were all situated around the kitchen table. "So, Gramps, what's so important you paid for two special deliveries to get us here?" Kylie asked around a mouthful of still-warm-from-the-oven, melt-in-your-mouth, grandmother cookies.

The jaunty smile faded from her grandfather's face, and Brendan sat forward, suddenly alert. "It's Mom, isn't it?" he said.

Gramps nodded. "It is, indeed."

Kylie gave a heavy sigh. "So it's time?"

Gramps nodded again. "I'm afraid so. We just don't seem to have any other choice." He pulled several folded sheets of paper from his pocket and smoothed them out on the table. "These are your assignments." He handed a sheet of paper to each of them.

Brendan and Kylie studied the papers thoughtfully. A grin broke out on Brendan's face. "Brilliant. Devious, but brilliant."

Kylie regarded her grandfather, new respect showing in her expression. "If I doubted it before, I won't do so again," she said. "Gramps, you are a genius."

"So," Gramps said, reaching out to lay his hands over those of his grandchildren. "It's unanimous. Operation Save Mom is officially begun."

ONE

Kitty's eyes opened slowly, as though acknowledging the new day was the last thing they wanted to do.

She couldn't blame them. She felt the same way. If only she could hide under the covers forever. But that wasn't possible.

Not with Kylie and Brendan and her parents hovering over her.

They were all so determined to help her, to cheer her up. It made her want to scream.

"Hope you're getting ready, Mom," her son, Brendan, had said a few days ago, that forced smile on his handsome face. "One more month until we *march* into April."

She knew he'd been trying to pull her from the doldrums, trying to push her into their family tradition of making April Fools' a day of fun and celebration and laughter. Ever since the children were small, March 1 had been, for their entire family, the starting date for "marching" forward and planning the biggest and best April Fools' caper in the world.

But what Brendan didn't know was that that very fact had triggered her depression. Yes, the other holidays since Dan's death had been difficult, but with her family's love and support, she'd managed to endure them. Rather admirably, she thought.

They'd even tried to make a go of last April Fools' Day. They'd all said the right things and done the right things, loath to admit it had been a dismal failure. Everything they did only seemed to emphasize Dan's absence.

She should have known it was a waste of time to even try. April Fools' had been *their* holiday. A tradition she and Dan started when they were dating and one they'd continued every year since. So when she'd glanced at the calendar last week and realized it was only ten days to March, then thought about how April was on its way…then April Fools' would be here again, the third one without her husband…a bone-deep weariness she'd never felt before had settled over her. Rather than the joy and anticipation of previous years, all she could feel was the bleak awareness of how horribly different April 1 would be from now on.

Of course, it only made matters worse that April 1 was also Dan's birthday. And the day they got married.

It was so fitting. Dan was a man who knew how to live with enthusiasm and joy. They'd both felt it was a fitting start to their marriage as well. And it had been. Most days their household had been steeped in "buffoonery and tomfoolery," as Dan loved to call it.

It was a well-known fact: Let a practical joke take place in the Hawk household, and Dan was as often the instigator as Kylie or Brendan. Kitty enjoyed a good prank, of course, but it was usually as a spectator.

Or a victim.

A memory shoved its way into her mind, an image so clear and distinct she felt she could almost reach out and touch it.…

She had come up the stairs from the basement, walked into the living room, and found herself in the middle of a fierce water fight.

Water dripped from the curtains and dribbled down the TV screen. A small pool was forming on the floor, held in check only by the cotton rug in front of the now-soggy couch. Her six-foot-three, forty-year-old husband was crouching behind the couch, full Super-soaker in hand.

"Daniel Willia—!" she bellowed, only to have the words cut short when what had to be an entire glass of water hit her full in the face.

Horrified silence filled the room for an instant, then, "Way to go, genius. You just creamed Mom."

"Me? I didn't cream her! You did!"

"Not a chance. That was your signature idiocy, runt."

She turned to glare at her elder child, her only son, Brendan, her firstborn, the one who was her constant ally in the onslaught of life...and was struck by the cheeky grin of delight on his face.

"Yo, Mom, gotta learn to duck," he remarked, holding out a handful of damp paper towels with a rueful shake of his head.

"No, I need to *be* a duck," she muttered as she snatched paper towels and tried ineffectually to stem the stream of water dripping from her hair and off the tip of her nose.

An arm slid around her shoulders, and she glanced up at Dan's face, which was adorned in his most winning smile. He didn't have a drop of water on him.

"Don't even try," she warned him.

"I think you'll find this is more effective." He held a dry towel out to her.

She stared at it, not moving. Another drip fell from her nose.

"You'll feel better if you dry off," he urged softly, tender humor evident in his voice.

She hated it when he did that, talked to her in that low, sweet tone when she wanted to be outraged. He knew his laughter was one of her greatest weaknesses.

Kitty looked away. "Forget it, Don Juan," she said. "You aren't getting off so easily." She spread her hands toward the room. "What do you think this is? The lost city of Atlantis?"

He looked properly chastised—or he tried, anyway, but the twinkle in his hazel eyes belied his penitent demeanor. A rebellious swath of thick, honey brown hair fell down on his forehead, and she fought the urge to reach out and brush it back.

"How did you stay so dry?" she grumbled.

"I learned to duck," he replied.

"Told you so, Mom," Brendan crowed.

She shook her head. "This room will be cleaned up," she asserted firmly.

"Yes, dear."

"And it will not be used for water fights in the future."

"Yes, Mom," her three troublemakers replied in chorus.

She took the towel from Dan, dried her face with it, and then dropped it back into his still-outstretched hand. She met his laughing gaze and smiled sweetly. "And you will take me out to the restaurant of my choice to help me recover from the trauma I've suffered."

His slow smile warmed her from head to toe. "It would be my pleasure."

No, she thought as the sound of his voice, low and loving, echoed in her mind. *No, the pleasure was all mine. And now it's gone....*

How exactly did one endure a birthday when the guest of honor was dead?

Fresh pain swept over her, and she rolled to her side, pulling the pillow over her head. "I can't do this anymore," she moaned to no one in particular. At least she told herself it was to no one. She absolutely, positively was *not* mumbling to God. Why bother? He had clearly stopped listening to her.

Otherwise, her husband would still be alive. Wouldn't he?

Despair slid into the bed beside her, covering her as completely as the blanket she was clutching. She squeezed her eyes defiantly against the tears that pushed to escape.

She didn't want to cry. She was tired of crying. She'd already cried a river. No, an ocean. No, *three* oceans. She gave a hoarse chuckle. How could one body hold so much water?

Get ahold of yourself, Kitty! her mind scolded her. *It's been two years now. Twenty-four months. Seven hundred thirty days.*

And every day had been a struggle. Oh, she got up each morning—well, most mornings, anyway—and took part in the business of living. But it wasn't the same. When Dan was alive, they'd relished their days together. They'd loved to go places. Whether on trips or just to the park or the library, they found things to do and enjoy. But without him…

Without him, Kitty was finding fewer and fewer reasons for going anywhere. Or for getting up in the morning. Dan used to tease her about being such an early riser. Sleeping in was not getting up until 6:00 A.M. Now she could hardly drag herself out of bed by ten. Or, on days like today, by noon.

Dan would be ashamed of you if he saw you like this! that same scolding voice nagged at her. *Get on with your life.*

Kitty clenched her fists. She wanted to hit something. She'd heard that from so many well-meaning friends and family members. "Get on with your life." But no one could answer the question that continued to scream in her head: *What* life? What kind of life was left for her without the husband who had filled her days with love and laughter since she was eighteen? Nearly thirty years.

Twenty-eight, to be exact, she told herself. *We were married for twenty-eight years.* And in all that time, he'd only made her cry twice: four years ago, when he told her he had cancer, and then the end of March, two years ago, when he died.

It had seemed to Kitty's grief-dazed mind the most unbeatable and horrible April Fools' joke of all.

The first April after Dan's death, they'd all been so engulfed in grief none of them had even noticed April 1 until the day was long gone. Last year…well, that disaster was most likely at least a part of why it had hit her with such force this year. And now all she wanted to do was hide. Or run. Or both.

She wished she could be different. That she could follow Dan's lead and go on to face life with anticipation. He had been a firm believer in the power of prayer and joy and laughter. "I know who's in control," he often said, even with his disease, "so why should I get discouraged?"

True to his words, he hadn't granted discouragement entrance into his heart or his home. Not once. Not in the midst of pain, not in the face of death. Amazingly, even as she was losing him, he'd filled Kitty's days with laughter. With a gentle humor and remarkable mimicry skills, he had regaled her with tales of the nurses, the doctors, and the other patients.

"There's so much joy all around us, Kitty," he told her on their last day together. "Don't ever forget that. Laughter is a gift from God because he loves you so much. Don't let go of it. And don't let go of love." His weary eyes had rested on her, full of love. "Don't turn away from love when it comes again."

She'd assured him she would not. But even as she said the words, they stuck in her throat. Love again? How would that be possible when her very heart was dying? No, she'd known as she said good-bye that her days of loving, laughing, dreaming…they were over.

Laughter. Dreams. God. Those were the things that made up who Dan was. Those were the things that Kitty had lost.

I am with you.

The words whispered through her mind, striking deep within her. She wanted to embrace them, to draw on them as a drowning man would draw on a tank of oxygen. But she couldn't. No, that wasn't true. She wouldn't.

I don't believe you. You aren't with me. You can't be. You let Dan die.

The creaking of the door alerted Kitty that she wasn't alone any longer. "Mom?"

She didn't move or answer.

"Mom." The voice was closer now. Kylie. Sweet Kylie, their younger child. Kitty had always shared a special connection with Kylie.

"She's your daughter, through and through," Dan often said. Kitty couldn't argue. For one thing, Kylie and Kitty both were dreamers. "Creative types," Brendan called them, usually with an indulgent grin. "Lots of imagination and no common sense." Some might be insulted by that, but Kitty didn't mind it. As far as she was concerned, common sense was highly overrated.

Kylie also shared Kitty's deep love of animals. So much so that she'd studied veterinary medicine and was now one of the youngest—and most requested—vets at the local animal clinic. Kitty and Dan had been so proud of her.

As they'd been proud of their son. Brendan was a computer consultant. In fact, he owned his own consulting firm and was one of the rising stars in the field. "The next Bill Gates," Dan would say with a grin. "Hurry up and make a million, son, so your mother and I can spend it when we retire!"

And yet, for all their professional success, what had pleased Dan most about their children was that they lived lives of faith. Kitty and Dan had raised them to do so, but in a world where so many voices clamored for a child's attention, Dan had found it a special joy that his children stayed tuned to the voice of God.

"God's blessings to us have been abundant. And evident." It was Dan's favorite saying, especially when he was looking at or talking about their children.

"Mom?" Kylie's voice came again, a bit more insistent this time.

Go away, she said mentally to Kylie. She didn't want to talk to anyone. *Go away. I'm asleep.* To prove it, she gave as realistic a snore as she could manage.

Her only reward was a snort of disbelief. "Nice try, Mom, but my room was next to Brendan's, remember? There's no way I'd buy that for a real snore. The walls aren't shaking." Her voice gentled. "Come on, Mom. I know you're awake, so you might as well come out."

Kitty gritted her teeth and pushed the pillow away, peering at her daughter. "I thought I taught you children to be polite," she muttered. "Can't you see I'm…resting?"

Quick sorrow filled her daughter's eyes, and Kitty felt a stab of guilt. But she pushed it aside. Why should she feel guilty? Didn't she have the right to her grief?

She started to say as much to Kylie when her daughter turned and walked toward the window, her steps firm and determined. "Kylie," Kitty said, hoping to stop her, but her daughter didn't pause.

"Looks like you forgot to open the curtains, Mom. You always told us you couldn't stand a room without sunshine." She took hold of the curtains and pulled them back, letting the light pour into the dark room.

"Don't," Kitty protested, but either Kylie had suddenly developed an acute case of deafness or she was simply ignoring

Kitty. She didn't even break her stride as she moved to the second window and set the daylight loose there as well.

Frustrated, Kitty pushed herself into a sitting position. "Kylie," she said more firmly.

"Boy, what a beautiful day," Kylie remarked conversationally, acting for all the world as though Kitty hadn't spoken. "A good day for the park."

"Kylie," Kitty's tone was growing ominous now.

Again, the words seemed to have no effect whatsoever. Kylie gave her a bright smile, pulled the curtains back on the last window, and then moved back to the doorway of the room.

"There you go," she said proudly, as though she'd just done Kitty some enormous favor. A quick, cutting retort jumped to Kitty's mind, but before she could let it loose, Kylie lifted what looked like an animal carrier from the floor and plopped it onto the bed.

"Anyway, I just stopped by to ask you a favor," Kylie said, opening the fasteners on the carrier.

"What—?" Kitty began, but she didn't get a chance to finish. Kylie had no sooner lifted the lid on the carrier than something small and furry darted out and dove under the covers.

"Awwwwk!" Kitty yelped, scrambling to get away from the beast. But it seemed to have decided she was someone it wanted to get to know. With rapid movements, it crawled straight at her. She pushed back until she slammed into the headboard. Folding her knees up against her chest, she looked around frantically for a weapon with which to defend herself.

Suddenly she felt something grasp at and clamber up her nightgown-clad legs. A yelp clawed at her throat, but before she could give it voice the critter was there, perched on her knees, nose-to-nose with her. A pair of clever little eyes—small, black, and beady—scrutinized her with what appeared to be keen interest. A small, pink nose twitched rapidly, whiskers all atremble.

Kitty stared in horrified silence for a second, then exploded from the bed with a screech. "A rat? You put a rat in my bed?" She flattened against the wall. "Kylie Renae, have you gone stark-raving mad?"

"Mother!" Kylie cried in scolding tones. "You frightened him!"

"I—!" Kitty stared at her daughter as though she'd turned purple. *"I frightened him?"*

Kylie didn't respond. She was busy looking under the covers, then under the pillows. Finally, she peered inside one of the pillows, and a grin broke over her features. "There you are," she cooed, reaching down to scoop the animal up. She cradled the long, furry body against her and gave Kitty a lopsided grin.

"He's not a rat, Mom," she said, holding the animal up for her mother's perusal. "He's a ferret."

Kitty looked more closely, then pinned her daughter with a glare. "You'll have to forgive me—" the words were laced with sarcasm—"I left my field guide in my other nightgown."

Kylie chuckled. "You've seen ferrets before, Mother. We watched a special on the Discovery Channel about them, remember?"

"I remember they're weasels," Kitty said, not budging from the wall. The ferret hung from Kylie's hands, looking every inch a weasel. But, Kitty had to admit, a very cute, very patient weasel.

Its long, sleek body and bushy tail dangled loosely as it turned its head this way and that, taking in its surroundings. Its little paws were cupped over Kylie's fingers and folded over each other, almost as though it were praying. Its coloring actually

21

was similar to that of a raccoon, with black and gray and white in the fur. It even had a black "bandit's mask" of color across its sharp little eyes.

A disturbing realization hit Kitty. A few years ago, Kylie had brought home a hedgehog. "They're all the rage for apartment pets," Kylie had said with a smile. Kitty recalled how delighted and intrigued she'd been—how she'd gone right over to pet the little animal, laughing at its antics. But now...

She closed her eyes wearily. Now she just didn't have the energy. So she stood there, not moving, not speaking, until Kylie spoke softly beside her, "Go ahead and pet him. He's really soft."

Kitty opened her eyes to find Kylie standing beside her, holding the ferret out to her. She wanted to refuse, to tell her daughter she saw right through her, that she was not going to get to her through this little bit of a fur ball...but she held her tongue, loath to wipe the hope from her younger child's face. With a resigned sigh, Kitty reached out a tentative hand.

The ferret watched her every move, sniffing at her finger as she touched its fur. Kylie was right; he was soft. Surprisingly so. She felt a smile tug at her lips as one little paw came to curl around her finger and a tiny, sandpaper tongue darted out to lick the fingertip.

Kitty met her daughter's laughing gaze. "Okay, so he's not a rat," she allowed grudgingly.

"And?" Kylie never had learned how to leave things alone.

"And he's cute."

Kylie grinned at that, then cradled the ferret in one arm and took hold of Kitty's nightgown sleeve with her free hand. "Come over here." She tugged her mother toward the chair near the window. Kitty followed her insistent daughter, sitting in the chair as she was urged. "Here," Kylie said, handing her the ferret.

"Wait—" she started to protest, but Kylie gently settled the small animal into her arms. Kitty stiffened, waiting for it to bolt, but it just sniffed, then curled into a warm, furry ball, its tail draped over its pink nose, and gave a deep, contented sigh.

Kitty felt her heart melting. "So what's this favor you need to ask?" she asked as she reached out one finger to scratch the little head between the ears.

"He needs a home."

Kitty looked up in quick refusal, but Kylie held her hand up, forestalling the objection. "Not for good, Mom. Just…for a while. His name is Bosco. A family brought him in a couple of months ago because they couldn't keep him. I thought he'd find a home quickly, but he hasn't." Kylie looked down at the now sleeping ferret. "We've all had fun with him at the clinic, so he's gotten lots of handling, which is good. But Dr. Dupuis told us yesterday that we can't keep him any longer, that we need to find a shelter for him."

"Why don't you keep him?"

Kylie shook her head. "One doesn't keep a ferret in the same home with Siberians, Mom. They'd think I'd brought home an hors d'oeuvre. I did check into possible ferret shelters or rescues in this area, but there don't seem to be any. I'd hate to see him destroyed. He's really a neat little guy."

Just then Bosco stretched, opened his mouth wide for a heartfelt yawn, then rolled onto his back and snuggled into the protective circle of Kitty's arms. His front paws were folded together, making him look as though he, too, were begging her for help.

Stop that! Kitty silently scolded him. *Stop being adorable. You are not going to make me like you.*

"Please, Mom," Kylie begged. "You might even decide you enjoy him…or want to keep him." She gave Kitty her most appealing look. It was perfect: a combination of puppy eyes and little-kid entreaty. And it worked every time.

Even now…even when Kitty's mind screamed at her to push the sleeping bundle of fur back into her daughter's arms, even when her heart cried out that it was too sore to care about anything…it worked.

"For how long?"

Kylie's face lit with triumph. "A few weeks. A month at the most."

"At the *most*," Kitty echoed firmly. "And just for the record, I won't want to keep him."

Her daughter leaned down to plant a kiss on her cheek. "Whatever you say, Mom." She sailed to the door. "And thanks. I'll go get his stuff from my car."

Kitty looked up. "Stuff? A ferret has stuff?"

"Oh, sure," Kylie answered breezily. "A cage, his toys, litter-box, his leash and halter—"

"Leash?" Kitty looked down at the animal. "For what?"

Kylie smiled a slow, victorious smile. "Walks, of course. At least once a day." Her smile broadened. "Good thing the park is so close, huh?"

"Now wait a minute! I never agreed to go to the park!"

But her daughter wasn't there to respond. She was out the door, bounding down the stairs, singing "Oh, What a Beautiful Morning" as she went, drawing out the last line: *"Ev'*-rything's *go*-ing my waaaaay."

Kitty settled back in the chair with a snort. "Little monster," she said, undecided whether she was referring to the ferret or her daughter.

∿ ∿ ∿ ∿ ∿

It didn't take long for Kylie to coax Kitty to get dressed and come help her set up the cage in the living room. Together they got Bosco settled into his new home.

Make that his temporary home, Kitty insisted to herself. *He's not staying.*

"This is his food. These are his toys. He loves bananas as a treat, but don't give him too much," Kylie said as she handed Kitty a book on Ferrets, then headed for the door. "And give me a call if you have any questions or problems. But I doubt you will. I think you two will get along great."

"Hmm," Kitty replied noncommittally, turning to look at Bosco, who was even now happily exploring his new digs. A sudden rush of panic hit Kitty. Why had she let her daughter talk her into this?

"Kylie, wait! I don't think—"

But she was gone. The sound of her car starting up and driving away gave the ring of finality to the situation. No getting out of it now.

She picked up the book on ferret care and went to watch Bosco as he pushed his way under the towel Kylie had put in the cage for him, then explored the small cloth hammock hanging from the top of his cage.

The animal had more sleeping arrangements than she did, for heaven's sake.

"So, temporary roomies, eh?" she said, reaching a finger in to scratch him behind his tiny ears. "Here's hoping we both survive it."

Brendan's car phone jangled as he sat waiting for a red light. He picked it up, but before he could say anything, the caller spoke.

"Red Toad, this is Blue Dog. Phase one of the mission has been implemented. You're authorized to begin phase two."

He looked to the roof of his car. "And you're authorized to go to the nut house," he said.

Kylie laughed. "You just can't stand it that I'm more creative than you are. Wait'll you see what I did for phase one."

Brendan knew his smile was as smug as his sister's tone of voice. "I'm sure you think you've done something brilliant, but let's not forget who the real genius is here."

"Yeah, right!" she exclaimed.

"Trust me on this one, dear Sister," he said with confidence. "Phase two is gonna knock your socks off."

"It's not my socks that need knocking off," she replied. "It's Mom's."

Brendan started to chuckle with wicked delight. "It's in the bag, Kyle," he said, using his childhood nickname for her. "Phase two is a guaranteed success."

TWO

Kitty leaned back against the cushions of the couch.
She loved this couch. She and Dan had picked it out
together. They'd hunted for weeks to find just the
right one. When they discovered this couch at one of the finer
establishments in town, they'd made sure it was comfortable
enough by lying down on it. In the showroom.

Of course, they'd taken their shoes off first. Didn't want to
get it dirty.

Warmth filled her at the memory, followed by quick surprise. For the last several months, such memories had brought
a pang of pain and loss. This time, it only brought a sense of
gratitude for all she and Dan had shared.

A clattering sound drew her attention, and she glanced over
at Bosco. Relief swept over her. He was right where he should
be, in his cage, playing with his water dish.

In the week since Kylie had deposited the animal into
Kitty's life, he'd escaped his cage twice. How, Kitty had yet to
fathom. She smiled at him in self-satisfaction. "Well, you won't
get out again," she said. She'd put extra fasteners on the door.
That should keep him in place.

At least, she certainly hoped so since she'd learned of late
that few things were as difficult to find as a ferret that didn't
want to be found. It was amazing the places that animal could
hide. His most recent trick had been to chew a hole through
the fabric on the bottom of the sofa and crawl inside.

"He's a burrowing animal, Mom," Kylie had explained when she came to get him out. "It's instinct."

"So is saving my sofa!" Kitty had responded firmly.

"Mom, if he's getting to be too much trouble, I can find someone else to watch him," Kylie had offered slowly.

Kitty had surprised them both by reaching out to take the squirming animal from her daughter. "That won't be necessary," she said, going to put Bosco back in his home.

"Oh?" Kylie's tone of voice positively oozed self-satisfaction. "Starting to like the little guy, eh?"

"Don't be silly," Kitty said, arranging Bosco's towel around him and giving him a scratch behind the ears. "I promised my darling daughter I'd help her out, and I simply have no desire to go back on that." She turned to smile at Kylie as benignly as possible. "No more, no less."

"Uh-huh." That was all Kylie had said, but Kitty had seen the glimmer of triumph and mirth in her daughter's eyes.

"Well, let her believe what she wants," Kitty said to Bosco. "I know the truth, and that's all that matters."

Bosco responded by coming to the side of the cage and going up on his hind legs, staring at her like a criminal begging to be freed from prison. "Oh no you don't, you rascal," Kitty said, laughing. "You just stay where you are."

He continued to stare at her, his beady little eyes seemingly filled with pleading.

"Oh, all right, then," Kitty relented. "You can go for a ride later."

She shook her head with a laugh. She had to admire the little guy. For all that he barely weighed three pounds, he didn't know the meaning of fear. He loved to ride around on Kitty's shoulder as she walked through the house. Generally, he was content to drape himself around her neck, like a living fur collar. But from time to time, he'd get what her mother used to call "a wild hare," and make a kamikaze leap from her shoulder to whatever surface was handy.

The first time he'd done this he'd scared the wits out of Kitty. Fortunately, he'd landed on the couch, so no damage had been done. But she had started putting his harness and leash on him whenever he was on her shoulder. Just for safety's sake.

He also loved to race around the house at top speed, zipping this way and that. He would run up to her, then back up, bobbing his head back and forth, making the most hilarious sounds.

She hadn't laughed so much in weeks as she had while watching the little scamp's antics.

"But I'm not starting to like you," she insisted through her grin. "Not even a little."

Just then the phone rang. It was Brendan. "Yo, Mother mine. Just wanted to let you know I called the repairman."

Kitty frowned in confusion. "Repairman? For what?"

"For the various and sundry things you've been asking *me* to fix for months now. Like I have the foggiest notion what to do about a dripping faucet or a toilet that runs on and on and on—"

"Not part of a computer genius's job description, dear?"

He laughed. "Definitely not."

"Brendan, is a repairman really necessary?" She cringed at the sound of a whine in her tone, but the thought of some stranger hanging around, even if it *was* to fix her faucet, didn't exactly thrill her. "In fact, I think I'm getting used to the drip. It's…" She paused. What would sound like a plausible reason for not fixing a dripping faucet? "Soothing." Of course. That was possible, wasn't it? "I kind of like listening to it at night." She smiled at what she felt was a clever diversionary tactic.

"Right, Mom."

Her smile faded. He wasn't buying it.

"Don't worry, the guy is reasonably priced and highly dependable. He's a nice old guy. His wife died some twenty years ago, Pastor David said. The man comes highly recommended. He joined the church six months ago or so. You'll like him, I'm sure."

A stab of guilt pierced her. She hadn't been to church in months. Now some little old man would be hanging around, talking about it, holding a mirror up for her to see how far she'd fallen from the days when Dan was alive. "Brendan, really—"

"Great! It's settled. He's coming this afternoon, so keep an eye out for him. His name is Kartz. Or Krantz. Or something like that."

"But I—"

"Okeydokey, Mom. Talk to you later. Love you!"

The dial tone sounded in Kitty's ear, and she held out the receiver, staring at it as though it had come to life. First the ferret, now a repairman. How was it her children were so convinced they knew better than she did what—and whom—she would like?

A rattle of wire drew her attention back to Bosco, who was shoving his food dish around with his nose. "Well!" Kitty said as she dropped the receiver into place. "How do you like that? It's my house, and I'm being told who—" she glared at him— "and *what* is coming over." She went to stand by the cage, her arms crossed. "Well, you and this Mr. Krantz may get in the door, but neither one of you is staying long." With that determined declaration, she stomped over and flopped onto the couch again, picking up the book on ferret care and opening it. "So don't bother getting too comfortable, my fine, furry, beady-eyed little friend. This is a temporary arrangement. Just keep that in mind."

Bosco paused, looking at her as though he were considering her words, then suddenly exploded into action. He bounced forward, then bobbed back and forth, shaking his head from side to side and making the oddest noise.

Alarm swept her, and Kitty jumped up and rushed to the cage. "Are you okay?" *Please, please, don't let anything happen to him.*

The desperation of her inner plea startled her—and disturbed her. But a quick study told her the ferret wasn't in any pain or distress. In fact, he looked as though he were dancing.

Bosco chirped. No, it wasn't a chirp. It was more like a grunt. Like a little pig grunt…like a very happy little pig grunt.

Kitty narrowed her eyes. "What in the world are you doing?" she demanded.

Bosco stopped his crazy dance, looked up at her, then came to the side of the cage and sniffed at her. His eyes were wide and curious, and he looked for all the world as though he were saying, "Hey there, don't worry; be happy!"

Kitty shook her head. "I never should have let Kylie talk me into this. I'm just not up to it!" she said fiercely. Bosco's only response was to walk over to his hammock, sniff it thoroughly, then climb in and curl up with a deep sigh.

Kitty stood there, watching him, wishing she could be so content, so at peace. Suddenly words drifted into her mind: *I am with you.*

The words rolled over her, through her, deep within her. She tried to work up the anger, to fight against the reassurance as she'd done every time God's Word had come to her since Dan's death. But she couldn't. There was something stirring within her, something flaring into life as she watched Bosco's deep, even breathing and peaceful repose. He had no control over his life. He was at the mercy of those around him who decided if he lived or died…and yet he was at peace.

He's an animal! He hasn't got the brainpower to be afraid! a mocking voice within her jeered.

That was true enough, but she realized the ferret had something else working for him. Instinct. All animals could tell instinctively if they were in trouble. Or if they were safe. And Bosco clearly sensed he was in caring hands.

So what? So an animal feels safe with you. What does that mean?

Kitty wasn't sure. Not exactly. But there was something rumbling around in her mind…something about trust and faith and knowing instinctively that she was safe in eternal, caring hands.

"'Your unfailing love, O Lord, is as vast as the heavens.'" The psalm, long a favorite of hers, came to her like a tide, and she recited it in a whispered voice. "'Your faithfulness reaches beyond the clouds. Your righteousness is like the mighty mountains, your justice like the ocean depths.'" Tears slowly found their way down her cheeks. "'You care for people and animals alike, O Lord. How precious is your unfailing love, O God! All humanity finds shelter in the shadow of your wings…for you are the fountain of life, the light by which we see.'"

I am with you.

Raw emotion washed over her, crashing like an ocean wave on the rock that had been her heart, wearing it down until the sharp, rough, angry edges finally, painfully, began to smooth.

"Oh, Jesus," she whispered. At the heart cry, light was set loose within her. It was as though…she let go a deep sigh…as though she were coming home.

Her gaze drifted back to Bosco, who was now fast asleep, lying on his back, his head dangling over the side of the hammock, the very tip of his pink tongue sticking out of his mouth. Kitty chuckled through her tears.

"I sure had you pegged wrong," she said to the sleeping animal. "Here I thought you were an intruding little weasel." She smiled. "Turns out you're an emissary from God." She expelled a soft breath of amazement. "Who would have figured that?"

She went back to the couch. Flopping against the cushions, she grabbed the ferret book and opened it up. "Okay, let's get down to business."

It took only a moment of squinting at the page to realize she needed more light. She leaned over to turn on the lamp, but her hand paused in midreach. There, next to the lamp on the end table, was Dan's Bible. It had sat in that spot, untouched, since his death. Oh, she'd dusted it—she didn't want it to look unused—but that was all. She'd refused to open it. Or to open her own Bible, which was put away in a drawer upstairs.

I am with you.

Biting the side of her mouth, Kitty turned on the lamp.

I am with you.

She laid her hand on top of the Bible, fingering the worn, well-used leather cover. She could still see the way Dan's hands had held the Bible as he read it.

I am with you.... I will give you peace.

Kitty closed her eyes. Peace. How she longed for peace, for the sense of safety and shelter she'd known for so many years. How had she lost those feelings?

Because they were based on Dan. The answer came to her, soft and gentle, yet filled with power. The power of truth. Her security, her sense of being sheltered, even her faith had been based on Dan.

She drew in a steadying breath, then lifted the Bible. Settling back against the pillows, she stared at it for a moment.

"Okay," she said a second time, "let's get down to business."

THREE

rash! Bang!

C Kitty sat up with a jerk, sending the Bible flying to the floor. She blinked rapidly, trying to free her fogged mind. *Must have fallen asleep,* she thought groggily, then knelt to pick up the Bible.

Her hand landed on the newspaper, which was spread across the floor. Kitty paused, staring. She'd put the paper in a nice neat pile next to the couch. How had it gotten spread out—?

Crash!

"What in the world...?" She looked around, bewildered. Then she saw it. Bosco's cage was empty. Her mouth dropped open, and she stared at the cage, disbelieving.

"Oh no! Not again!"

Bang!

She jumped to her feet and started for the sound, sudden awareness hitting her. The living room looked like a tornado had hit it! The table lamp had been knocked to the floor. That must have been what woke her. But it wasn't the only evidence of the ferret's freedom. In addition to the paper and the lamp, couch pillows were scattered all about, as though someone had thrown them into the air in wild abandon.

Kitty clenched her teeth. "I hope you had fun, you little weasel, because the party's over." She looked around, then frowned. "At least, it will be when I find you."

Crash!

Kitty spun in the direction of the noise. The kitchen. The little dickens was in the kitchen.

She rushed into the room, and the sight that met her there stopped her cold. Her containers of flour, sugar, and salt had been knocked over, and there was a blanket of the three substances covering the room. What wasn't blanketed had tiny white ferret pawprints tracked across it. The dishes that had been stacked in the drainer to dry were scattered across the counter, and the window above the sink was now sporting a huge hole in the glass.

"Oh, Bosco!" Kitty wailed. Then she looked around the room. Speaking of the little devil, where *was* he?

A grunting sound drew her attention, and she turned and looked up....

There, atop the refrigerator, whiskers and paws covered with flour, was Bosco. He bobbed his head, backing up and chattering gaily as though to say, "See, Mom? Look what I did for you!"

Kitty lunged at the ferret, and he squealed and scampered off the fridge and down onto the countertop.

"Bosco! Come!" Kitty bellowed. Either Bosco didn't know "come" or he simply didn't care to respond. Whatever the situation, he didn't even break his rapid stride as he scrambled across the kitchen counter. Kitty went after him, but the flour on the floor made it slick. Without warning, her feet suddenly shot out from under her, and she landed with a thump on her back.

Dazed from the fall, she stared up...and found a furry little face staring back at her. Bosco was balanced on the edge of the sink, peering at her, his nose whiskers twitching crazily.

Ignoring the twinges of pain, Kitty reached up slowly, slowly…

Bosco lunged, springing from the sink and landing right in the middle of Kitty's prone form. She yelped, then grabbed at him, but the ferret was already gone, scampering across the kitchen floor and into the living room, chattering all the way.

Kitty scrambled to her feet and went in hot pursuit.

"Bosco, you little rat!" she yelled, which only seemed to spur the ferret into greater speed. He dashed around the room, leaving little white pawprints all over Kitty's blue carpeting. She followed his lead, over the fallen lamp, around the couch, through the potted floor plant, and then…he scooted under the couch.

"Oh no!"

That couch weighed a ton! The last thing Kitty wanted to have to do was lift it up to grab her little escapee.

Just then, the doorbell rang.

"Brendan, where are you when I need your muscle?" Kitty wailed as she went to pull the door open.

"Mrs. Hawk?"

Kitty stared for a moment, then clapped her hands together. "Wonderful! A man! Just what I need." She reached out to grab the front of the man's jacket and pull him inside.

"Excuse me?" He stared at her, wide eyed.

"Hurry! Over here!" She tugged him toward the couch.

"Whoa, lady, I'm just the repairman!"

She turned to regard him, and the shock on his face stopped her. The sudden awareness of what she'd said and how it must have sounded to him brought a rush of heat to her face. "Oh, my! No, no, no! When I said I needed a man I didn't mean—" She broke off, mortified. This was awful! "That is, I wasn't asking you—well, not exactly…What I mean is, well…" her voice trailed off weakly.

"What—" he looked from her to the couch—"*did* you mean? Exactly?"

Her answer was cut off by a now-familiar baby-pig grunt. Kitty spun to stare at Bosco, who had come out from under the couch and was standing there, watching them.

"Shhhh!" Kitty hushed the man, planting her palm against his chest to ensure that he didn't move. "Don't spook him!" She hissed.

Too late.

At the sound of her voice, Bosco did his ferret fandango, then dashed back under the couch.

"Oh, drat!" Kitty wailed. She looked at the repairman, then had to bite her lip to keep from laughing at the expression on his face.

"That was a weasel," he said in clear disbelief.

"Not quite," Kitty corrected. "Bosco is a ferret."

The man turned to study her, and she was suddenly aware of very blue eyes, a thick mane of silvery hair, and a strong, square, clean-shaven jaw. He was tall and strongly built. Fiftyish, if she didn't miss her guess. She felt her forehead crease in confusion. Where was the doddering old gentleman Brendan had told her about? This man was…oh my. He definitely was *not* doddering.

"I take it your ferret doesn't belong under the couch?"

"My…what?" she asked, still caught in her study of the man.

A faint glint of humor touched his ice-blue eyes, and he arched a brow.

"Oh!" she looked away, mortified. "Of course, my ferret. Bosco." She shook her head. "No, he doesn't belong under the couch." She looked back at him, all business now. "That's where you come in."

He nodded. "You need me to lift the couch."

She smiled. "Bingo."

He inclined his head. "Well, then, let's see what we can do."

Jericho walked toward the couch, wondering what he'd gotten himself into. Kitty Hawk wasn't at all what he'd been expecting. For one thing, she was considerably younger than her son had led him to believe.

"My mother's a widow," Brendan Hawk had said over the phone, sounding all doting indulgence and concern. "She's recovering from my father's death two years ago, and, well, she's grown rather frail. And a bit feeble at times. She really can't manage the house, but she can't bear to leave it. Or the memories it still holds. I'm really very concerned about her."

Upon hearing this, Jericho had leaned back in his chair with a sigh. He shouldn't take the job. He knew that. His calendar was already full. But the image of a sweet little white-haired, elderly lady with a house full of repair needs got to him.

Besides, he could still remember how hard it had been when his wife, Alice, died more than twenty years ago. It had taken him a long time to feel as though he was on an even keel again.

"Okay," he said. "Give me the address." It would be a pain to shuffle his jobs, but he'd manage.

Now, watching Kitty Hawk as she knelt in front of the couch and peered beneath it, he realized he'd been had. Oh, she was little enough. Petite was the word. But elderly? Not hardly. And feeble? Well, he could already see that that word had nothing to do with this woman's physical state. As a matter of fact, though he figured she was close to his age—he knew her son was nearly thirty, so she most likely was close to fifty—she looked considerably younger.

Must be that wide-eyed expression of wonder on her face, he thought and smiled. He hadn't had a woman look him over with such evident fascination in a long time. Not that there weren't women interested in him. He was considered quite a catch, even at fifty. Or so he'd been told. But there had been something about her expression—something about the way her lips had parted and her cheeks had tinged with pink when she stood there studying him as though she were imprinting his image in her mind—that was almost as disconcerting as it was alluring.

Alluring?

"Whoa, buddy, get a grip!" he muttered, and she looked up at him.

"Excuse me?"

"I said are you ready to get a grip on him?"

She nodded. "I think so."

Nice save, Katz, ole boy, he congratulated himself. "Okay, here we go."

He took a deep breath, bent at the knees, and hefted one end of the heavy couch. *Good thing I was here,* he thought. *She never would have—*

"Hey!" he yelped as something grasped at the bottom of his pants leg. *"Hey!"* he repeated on a roar as that something scampered up his leg, *inside* his pants.

"Look out!" the "feeble" widow yelped, jumping out of the way as he dropped the couch.

"Get this thing off me!" he bellowed, reaching for his belt buckle.

"Wait!"

"Wait?" he hollered. "Are you nuts? I've got a ferret in my pants!"

"You can't take your pants off here!"

"Lady," he said in as controlled a voice as he could, "I've got a *ferret* in my *pants!* One of us has to get out. Now!"

She jumped up, grabbed his arm, and dragged him across the living room, then shoved him into what looked like a guest bathroom near the front door.

He didn't even wait to see if she shut the door. He stripped his pants, dancing around frantically as the small creature clawed at his leg.

"Don't hurt him!" Kitty's muffled voice came through the doorway.

"Don't—!" he began, then clamped his lips shut. Unbelievable. Absolutely unbelievable.

He held his pants out in front of him, and there, clutching the material and swinging back and forth, was the infamous Bosco, tiny ears perked, whiskers twitching like mad, tail puffed out and looking like a bottle brush.

"Hello, weasel," he muttered.

"Don't frighten him!" came Mrs. Hawk's concerned voice again.

"Oh, heaven forbid," he said through clenched teeth. He reached out slowly, relieved when his hand closed around the trembling animal. "I have no intention of frightening him," he called through the door. "Fricasseeing, maybe," he grumbled. "But certainly not frightening."

A quick inspection of his legs revealed some minor scratches but nothing serious. He stepped toward the door, hiding behind it and opening it just enough to stick his hand out. "I believe this belongs to you."

"Oh, Bosco, you poor baby!" she exclaimed, snatching the animal from his hand. "Did he hurt you?"

Jericho stood there, leaning his forehead against the door. *This is a test, Lord, right? You've put me with a crazy woman as some kind of test?* He shoved the door closed with a quick, frustrated motion, then turned to open the medicine cabinet. Fortunately there was antiseptic cream there, and he applied it liberally to his leg, grimacing as it stung.

"Serves me right for not listening to my common sense," he groused, jerking his pants back on. "Next time, Katz, listen to yourself when you say you're too busy for something."

When he stepped out into the living room, Bosco was back in his cage, curled up in a small hammock, clearly exhausted from his ordeal.

"Are you all right?"

Jericho met the concerned gaze of the Widow Hawk and bit back a sarcastic response. "Fine," he said, proud of the even tone of his voice. *Stick to the business at hand, Katz.* "A few scratches, but that's it."

She came forward to place a small hand on his arm. "I'm so sorry!" she said. "I never dreamed he would…well…" She glanced back at the cage. "I'm watching him for my daughter. She's a vet. And he keeps escaping his cage."

So much for sticking to business. He glanced down at her hand where it still rested on his arm, surprised at how much he liked the feel of it there. She followed the direction of his gaze and snatched her hand away, stains of scarlet appearing on her cheeks as she stepped back.

Their gazes met and locked, and something stirred deep within him. He watched as emotions played across her attractive features. She had tiny wrinkles at the corners of her eyes, evidence that she smiled often. Her face was framed by shoulder-

42

length hair the color of aspen gold. There were streaks of white throughout it, which, in Jericho's eyes, only added a greater depth and beauty.

No, Kitty Hawk was definitely not elderly.

But it wasn't her refined beauty that captivated him. It was her eyes, for there was a shadow in their brown depths, a hint of some fathomless sorrow that wouldn't let her go.

Or that she wouldn't let go of...?

She found her voice first. "I take it you're Mr. Kratz?"

He wrenched himself away from his absurd preoccupation with her face and drew in a steadying breath. What was wrong with him? In the space of fifteen minutes, this woman had jerked him into her house, subjected him to becoming a jungle gym for a weasel, and accused him of hurting the beast that had tried to turn his leg into shredded wheat.

And yet he stood there, looking at her like a lovestruck loon, his brain turned to so much Malto Meal. This was not a good sign.

Katz, my man, he chided himself, *if you have any common sense left at all, you'll turn around and run away from here as fast as your legs can carry you.*

Kitty stood in silence, waiting for the man in front of her to respond. He had the oddest expression on his face. A kind of fascinated panic.... It reminded her of a deer caught in the headlights of a car.

"Not quite," he finally said, echoing her earlier correction of him. He took her proffered hand. "The name is Katz."

As much as she denied it, Kitty was acutely aware of the warmth and size of the man's hand as it engulfed hers. She hadn't reacted this way to a man since—

Quick shame filled her. *Dan, oh, Dan, I'm sorry.* She shouldn't be feeling like this!

"Jericho Katz," he went on.

She looked up at him with interest. "Jericho?"

He held up his hands as though to hold off her comments. "I know, I know, not your run-of-the-mill name. What can I say? My parents held an inordinate fondness for the Old Testament. My brother's name is Judah. My sister is—"

"Let me guess. Jezebel?"

He grinned. "Nice try, but no dice. Try Jochabed." He shook his head. "My parents loved being different."

"No more so than mine," she said, leaning against the back of the sofa. "My name is Kitty."

"Kitty Hawk," he said, and chuckled. "I see what you mean."

"That's my married name," she said, sharing in his amusement. "My maiden name was worse."

"You're kidding."

She shook her head. "Kohrner," she said with a laugh. "So I was Kitty Kohrner growing up. Believe me, I can relate."

"Kitty Kohrner," he echoed, saying the name slowly, as though relishing the sound of it. "Even better."

They shared a smile, and a warm rush of pleasure filled her at the look in his eyes.

Stop it! she scolded herself. What was wrong with her?

Don't turn away. The echo of Dan's words whispered through her mind, and she felt her heart constrict. No, oh no. She wasn't ready. She shook her head. No, she wasn't attracted to this man...not like *that!* Her reaction had to be because it was so rare to find someone who didn't find her name completely bizarre.

She'd grown used to people reacting to her name with varying degrees of embarrassment or surprise. In fact, by the time she'd reached her teens, Kitty had been able to peg how people would react when they first heard her name. The most common responses were startled looks, amused grins, even double takes.

From there people generally went one of several ways. The most common comment was, "Oh, my. How…interesting." And, once in awhile: "Wow. So how long did it take you to forgive your parents?"

Kitty chuckled at the thought. Forgive her parents indeed. Thank them was more like it.

Kitty's parents were the anchor in her life, the two people she could always count on for unconditional love and support. They had taught her how to stand on her own, how to walk forward with confidence and faith, how to take life by a storm. They'd instilled in her the faith in God that had carried her through her most turbulent and painful times…like Dan's death.

"You'll come through this, Kitten," her father had told her just a few months ago. "God's got plans for your future. Plans that will bring you hope."

"I can't see it, Dad," she'd sobbed, and he'd wrapped his arms around her.

"That's okay. I'll see it for both of us."

Jericho Katz's deep voice brought her awareness back to him. "Let me guess. Your parents wanted to help you learn to laugh at yourself."

"Yes, as a matter of fact, they did." His insight surprised her. "How did you know?"

He lifted his shoulders in a careless shrug. "Mine, too." Wry amusement flickered in the eyes that met hers. "Are you sure we aren't long-lost brother and sister?"

A gamut of perplexing emotions ran through her, and she found it impossible not to return his disarming smile. "I sincerely doubt it," she said. If there was one thing her reactions to him had *not* been, it was sisterly.

Please, God, she pled. *Please tell me I'm not becoming a desperate old widow woman who's ready to waylay any man who comes her way.*

"Well," Jericho said, "it's refreshing all the same to meet someone else with a unique name." He glanced around the tousled room, then back at her. "Decorating courtesy of Bosco?"

She nodded. "Wait 'til you see the kitchen."

"Well, lead on, Mrs. Hawk. I'm all yours."

That casual comment—and the appealing image it created in her imagination—brought the warmth rushing back into Kitty's cheeks. She pushed away from the couch hastily. Jericho Katz was altogether too disturbing. If he was going to be around much—which was entirely likely, considering the number of things that needed to be done around the house—she was just going to have to conquer her involuntary reactions to him.

No matter how hard that might be.

FOUR

Kitty stood in the bathroom, staring at her reflection. "What's wrong with you?" she asked, frustrated.

She set the brush down with a clatter and went to flop in the chair near the window. For the last two weeks, since Kylie had brought Bosco into her life—and Brendan had brought Jericho Katz—she'd been fighting feelings of restlessness. It was as though there was something unfinished...something important she needed to be doing.

But what?

Lord, I'd appreciate a bit of help here.

Her quick prayer brought a smile to her lips. She'd been doing that a lot since the day she'd started reading Dan's Bible. Praying. Talking to God. She'd done it often enough during her life, but this felt different. More...personal. As though she was talking to someone she knew rather than to someone Dan knew. She hadn't realized it until this last week, but she'd always had the feeling, deep inside, that God only listened to her because she was with Dan. Now...

Now she had the sense of being heard, and loved, just for herself.

It felt good.

So why am I so unsettled?

It was a good question, but one for which she had no answer. She glanced at Dan's Bible—which she was starting to think of as her Bible now—where it lay on her nightstand. She went to pick it up and turned to the section of the book of John that she'd been reading early this morning.

"'Do you love me?...Then feed my lambs,'" she read out loud. The words seemed to resonate within her, and she realized her heart was pounding. She trailed her finger down the page, then read again. "'Do you love me? ...Then take care of my sheep.'"

Yes.

The affirmation rang within her, striking deep, stirring emotions she didn't fully understand. "What does it mean?" she asked, wanting to know more than she'd wanted anything in a long time.

Take care of my sheep.

She shook her head, confused, and set the Bible aside. A rattling sound came from downstairs, and she smiled. It was past time for Bosco's morning jaunt in the park. She stood and headed for the door.

Maybe some fresh air would help her clear her head. And her heart.

Kitty loved the park. During the last two years she'd almost forgotten how much she loved it.

But now that she was back, she found herself more aware than ever before of the restorative effect it had on her. There was something fresh and alive and rejuvenating in the park.

Why had she stayed away so long?

Because you didn't want to go on, to enjoy life, when Dan couldn't.

The truth hit her, and she stopped in her tracks. Bosco, however, kept going, until he hit the end of the leash and was jerked off his paws.

"Oh," Kitty said, "I'm sorry, fella."

Bosco jumped up and faced her, backing away in his little side-to-side jig and grunting. Clearly, he did not appreciate what had happened.

Smiling at the feisty little animal, Kitty started walking again, grateful that it was still early enough that there weren't a lot of people around. Over the last week she and Bosco had become park celebrities of sorts. There was something about walking a ferret on a leash that made people stop and stare.

The first time she came to the park, she'd come shortly after lunch, not realizing the stir her little companion would cause. She'd no sooner walked near the playground than a little boy stopped in midrun and stood there staring with open-mouthed, wide-eyed amazement. He watched Bosco bouncing along in that loping way of his; then the boy spun around and raced to his mother. He tugged excitedly on her jeans until she looked down at him. "Mommy!" he exclaimed, half in horror, half in wonder. "What happened to that lady's *dog?*"

Within minutes Bosco was the main playground attraction. Children gathered around, hunching down to watch Bosco and giggle with delight at his undulating walk. At first Kitty was mortified. Then a thought drifted into her mind, making her grin: Dan would have loved this! Suddenly she found herself laughing, talking with the children, and having a good time.

Now she looked forward to the morning walks she and Bosco shared. In fact, those walks were becoming one of the highlights of her day. Today, though, with troubling thoughts on her mind, Kitty hadn't paid attention to how far they were walking. Though they were stopped several times by curious passersby—one man practically fell off his bike when he saw Bosco, then did a U-turn and came to pet the happy ferret—it appeared that Bosco was tired.

Kitty figured this out when the little fellow plopped down on the ground and refused to move. After a few tugs on the leash with no response, Kitty laughed, then reached down to pick up the worn-out ferret.

"How about we take a rest, Bosco, my boy?" She glanced around, then headed for her favorite bench—the one facing the playground, where children swarmed over the equipment with abandon. She sat down, Bosco cradled in her arms, and settled in with a sigh.

She'd really been hoping a walk would help her see things more clearly. But she was no closer to understanding her inner struggle than she'd been before she left the house.

Take care of my lambs.

The phrase drifted into her mind again, and she shook her head. *What does that mean, Father? I don't understand.*

"May I join you?"

Kitty turned to see a small, elderly woman standing there. From the mosaic of wrinkles on her face, Kitty guessed the woman was in her late seventies. Her expression was warm and sweet, and her bright blue eyes twinkled with intelligence and humor. *Now that,* thought Kitty, *is the quintessential grandmother face.* Even the woman's garb reinforced the image of a sweet—albeit slightly eccentric—grandmother: a flowered blue dress topped with a pink sweater, elegant white gloves, and a broad-brimmed straw hat complete with a spray of silk lily of the valley.

Hanging from the little woman's arm was one of the largest straw purses Kitty had ever seen, and it was bulging.

No…it was *moving.*

Kitty sat up straighter on the bench, and the woman glanced at her, then her face lit with a beautiful smile.

"Why, you have a ferret!" she exclaimed. "How sweet."

Kitty smiled, pleased to meet someone who was apparently familiar with Bosco's sort. "Yes, he is sweet," she said, surprised to find she meant it. For all that he was a scamp, she really had enjoyed having the animal around. "His name is Bosco." She glanced down at the snoozing animal. "I'm afraid I wore him out this morning."

"Oh, my. I know how the little tyke feels," the woman said, nodding toward the bench. "May I?"

"Oh! Of course," Kitty said in a rush, her eyes fixed on the wriggling bag. "Please do."

The woman sat down with a sigh and set the bag at her feet. She turned to Kitty and extended her hand in a graceful motion. "May I introduce myself?" she asked, and Kitty caught the hint of a southern accent. "I am Lily DuPont—" she pronounced the name *Dew*-pont— "of the Richmond DuPonts." Two dimples appeared in her furrowed cheeks as she smiled with beautiful candor. "But my friends just call me Miss Lily."

Balancing Bosco in one arm, Kitty took Miss Lily's hand and was surprised by the strength of the small gloved fingers. "I'm Kitty," she said, "Kitty Hawk."

"Why, how utterly enchanting!" Miss Lily exclaimed, delight deepening the twinkle in her clear eyes. "How your parents must have loved you to gift you with such a delightful appellation."

"Yes," she said in answer to Miss Lily's comment. "Yes, my parents love me a great deal."

"If your tone of voice is any indication, I daresay you feel the same about them." Kitty had the distinct impression that her companion was pleased by this.

"Oh, I certainly do," Kitty replied, scratching Bosco behind the ears and settling back against the bench. "My parents are wonderful."

"Well, if their choice of a name for you is any indication, I would guess they are people of great vision and purpose." Miss Lily's bubbly voice all but overflowed with approval.

"They are that," Kitty agreed.

"I would guess you are, as well, my dear."

Kitty smiled gratefully at the small woman. "I'd like to be. In fact, that's part of the reason I'm here today."

"Oh?"

She smiled, feeling a bit self-conscious. "It sounds odd…"

"Not at all, dear. Go ahead."

"Well, I'm trying to decide what I want to be when I grow up." She gave Miss Lily a self-deprecating smile. The woman merely nodded encouragingly, so Kitty went on. "You see, my husband died two years ago—"

"Oh, I'm so sorry."

Kitty inclined her head. "Yes, I am, too. He was a wonderful man. He knew how to make a difference in people's lives. I thought I did, too, but I've recently realized I was just riding on his coattails, so to speak. Now I want to find what it is that *I'm* supposed to do. How I can make a difference in people's lives."

"A worthy quest, to say the least," Miss Lily said. The bag at her feet rustled again, and she looked down with an indulgent smile. Kitty glanced down at it curiously, watching with keen interest as Miss Lily reached down into the bag and cooed, "There now, Sweetums, Mummy's right here."

Kitty felt her eyes widen. Good grief. Was the poor woman delusional? As Kitty looked around to see if there was an attendant nearby, the woman sat up straight again and turned those bright blue eyes on her. Kitty forced a smile to her lips, then felt her mouth drop open in surprise.

There, in the woman's hands, cradled close to her flowered

52

bosom, was a small mass of fur and whiskers and pricked-up ears.

"Oh!" Kitty exclaimed, smiling at the silky terrier. "How adorable."

The woman smiled beatifically, as though she were holding the greatest treasure in the world. "This is my Sweetums," she said, her fingers tenderly scratching the silky's head, just behind its pointed ears. "She's a bit feisty, so you'll want to keep your little friend away from her, but she's a love all the same."

Kitty lifted her free hand toward the dog, then paused. The last thing she wanted was to suddenly find Sweetums attached to her hand or wrist. True, the dog was tiny—she couldn't weigh more than nine or ten pounds—but Kitty knew terriers were notorious for being ready to take on any opponent, regardless of size.

Kylie had told her once about a client at the clinic whose Yorkshire terrier was constantly getting out of the house. The woman's greatest concern wasn't that the dog would get lost, but that it would end up facing down a car.

"I can see it now," Kylie had recounted with a laugh. "There would be Dusty, standing in the middle of the road, staring at the car and thinking, *You're the biggest dog I've ever seen, but I think I can take you!*"

Kitty grinned at the memory, though it did make her cautious. "May I?" she asked Miss Lily, nodding to the dog.

Miss Lily inclined her head in a graceful motion. "Of course, my dear. Sweetums *loves* attention. Don't you, little one?"

As Kitty stroked the silken fur, the tiny dog leaned into her hand, tipping her head so that Kitty's fingers hit just the right spot. She grinned at Miss Lily, who gave her a conspiratorial wink.

"There, now, I knew you were trustworthy the moment I saw you. Sweetums has a highly refined sense of discernment." Kitty's grin widened at the definite note of pride in the woman's voice. "She can tell who is and isn't to be trusted." She leaned down to press her cheek against the dog. "Can't you, darling?"

Being the center of so much attention was sending Sweetums into ecstatic wriggles, and her stub of a tail wagged so furiously that Kitty thought it might fall off.

"Her discernment is further evident in the fact that she adores my children," Miss Lily said with a gratified smile. Then it was as though a cloud passed over her face. "If only my daughter weren't allergic to her." She sighed and looked at Kitty forlornly. "I rarely get to see my Eliza because of it. She lives too far away to come here often—her job simply doesn't allow for much time off. But I'm afraid I cannot bear the idea of leaving Sweetums in a kennel."

"Isn't there anyone who can watch her while you're gone?" Kitty asked.

Miss Lily shook her head. "I'm afraid not. Many of my friends can't have animals where they live, or they have pets of their own and couldn't manage two." She shook her head sadly. "I did call a few of those pet-sitting places, but all they do is come to your home to feed the animal and let it out twice a day. Why, Sweetums would be alone all day! That just wouldn't do."

Kitty sat up straighter, suddenly alert. She stared at the woman and her dog for a moment. Sweetums wasn't exactly a lamb, still…"What you need," she said slowly, "is someone who could take Sweetums in. In a home setting, not a kennel."

Miss Lily's face lit up. "Oh, that would be lovely. But finding someone like that, someone whom I could trust with my Sweetums, would be quite a task. Why, that person would have to be as honest as the day is long—"

"She'd have to love animals," Kitty added.

"She?" Miss Lily echoed, and Kitty grinned.

"To be nurturing," she said with a wink.

"Oh, of course," Miss Lily agreed. "And she'd have to have plenty of room, so the darling could run. A nice big house with a nice big yard."

"She'd need access to a vet, just in case there were problems," Kitty pointed out, excitement building within her.

"Absolutely, and she would have to be willing to treat Sweetums as if she were her very own."

"And you would pay for this kind of service?" Kitty asked.

Miss Lily looked at her, eyes wide. "For someone I could trust to care for Sweetums while I'm gone? Absolutely. As a matter of fact, I'm sure my friends with pets would feel the same. None of them likes to leave their darlings at kennels."

Oh, Father, Kitty's heart sang out, *this is it! I can tell. I can feel it's right.*

"May I ask you for your address and phone number?" Kitty said to Miss Lily. The woman regarded her for a moment, then nodded.

"Of course, my dear." She leaned over to rummage in her bag. "I believe I have a pencil and paper in here somewhere.... Ah. There we go." She lifted the items triumphantly, then handed them to Kitty and gave her the requested information.

Kitty folded the paper and slipped it into her pocket, then took Miss Lily's hand in hers. She wanted to lean over and give the woman a kiss but thought better of getting Bosco that close to Sweetums. No point in testing fate!

"You've been an enormous help to me," she told the older woman. "In fact, I think God sent you here today. Thank you so much."

Miss Lily's eyes sparkled with sudden tears. "No, my dear, thank you. And please, let me know how things turn out."

Kitty grinned. "Miss Lily, you can count on it!"

Jericho stepped back to survey his work with a satisfied smile. There was something so gratifying in putting things right that had gone wrong.

In this particular case, he'd just finished replacing the window that Bosco had demolished during his mad bid for freedom last week. Jericho shook his head. He wasn't sure who was crazier, Bosco or his owner.

Jericho had been working at Kitty's house for nearly a week now. He'd no sooner check off an item on her son's list, than her son—or Kitty herself—would add something else.

"You know, that garbage disposal hasn't been working quite right," Brendan had said when Jericho informed him he was almost finished.

"Would you mind terribly repairing the handrail on the stairway?" Kitty had asked that same day.

He shook his head. The only item left on the list now was the kitchen faucet, which shouldn't take any time at all. With any luck, this was his last day around Kitty Hawk.

You're a coward.

The accusation stung, but Jericho didn't deny it. "I don't need any complications in my life, okay?" he muttered, putting his tools away. "And if there's one thing this woman would be, it's a complication."

True, she was likable enough. Too likable, in fact. By far. All she had to do was come near him and Jericho felt his heart rate pick up speed. The way she looked, the sound of her voice, even that faint scent of vanilla that seemed to follow her everywhere…They were all getting to him.

So much so that every time she came around him, he turned into a walking disaster. Yesterday she'd come up behind him and asked what he was doing just as he was swinging his hammer. Startled, he missed the nail entirely. His thumb, however, was taught a severe lesson. As was the drywall the day she opened the front door as he was carrying a ladder through the room. He jumped back to avoid hitting her or the door. He succeeded, but the wall wasn't so lucky. He rammed it with the bottom of the ladder, knocking a hole the size of a watermelon in it. Then there was the time early in the week when she asked him if he wanted coffee. He turned to answer her and knocked his wrench off the counter. Fortunately it didn't damage the floor tile. Unfortunately that was because it landed on his foot.

If he was around her much longer, he'd end up on disability!

"Not only is she hazardous to my health, she drives me crazy," he told the pipes as he got ready to shut off the water. "She's about as organized as a teenager's bedroom. Her mind goes in forty different directions at once, and a single conversation can hit on a dozen different topics."

He shook his head. His late wife had been very much like him, and their life together had been uncomplicated and peaceful. There had been few surprises with Alice, but that had been fine with Jericho. As far as he was concerned, surprises were highly overrated. "No sir, this is one woman I can do without."

"Jericho?"

He jerked up, slamming his head on the pipes. "Youch!" he yelped, and she was suddenly there beside him.

"Are you okay?"

He lay there, staring up at the offending pipes. "Oh, sure,

I'm fine. No problem." His throbbing forehead disagreed, but he staunchly ignored it.

"Jericho, I was just wondering…"

He sighed heavily. She wasn't going to go away. "Hang on." As cautiously as possible, he slid out from under the sink, smiling when he completed the process without any further mishaps. He turned his head and found himself staring right into those warm, brown eyes. She was kneeling beside him. He stared at her, suddenly struck dumb.

God, help! The desperate prayer was all his dazed mind could manage. *I don't want to feel this way! My life is fine as it is. I don't need this. Please…*

"Jericho?" She reached out to touch his hand. "Do—"

The contact of her soft fingers against his hand shot through him like a jolt of electricity. He jerked his hand away and scrambled to his feet. In the back of his mind was the image of that crazy robot on *Lost in Space,* waving its wobbly arms and intoning, "Danger, Will Robinson! Danger!"

It's true, Father. I'm in danger…of losing my mind completely.

Your mind, or your heart? a voice from within countered.

"Shut up!" he muttered.

"What?"

He shook his head. "No, no, not you."

She looked around the room, totally bewildered, then stared at him as though he'd gone completely loony. Well, maybe he had. He shoved his hands into his pockets. "You were wondering?" he prompted.

Her eyes lit up, and she stood, clapping her hands together like a child at a birthday party. "Oh! Yes. I was wondering, do you do renovations?"

Warning bells sounded in his brain again. As casually as he could manage he said, "Well, yes, I do. Why?"

Her smile was eager and alight with excitement. "I want to make some changes on my house."

"Changes?"

She nodded enthusiastically. "I'm going to start my own business."

The idea of this whimsical woman running a business made his head pound. *She'll lose her shirt, God!* he protested.

Take care of my lamb, came the reply.

Oh no! This wasn't his responsibility. *She* wasn't his responsibility. He was not in the market to be someone's caretaker. Not even if that someone was as tantalizing as the Widow Hawk was!

"Sounds pretty ambitious," he said dryly.

"Oh, it is," she agreed. "But it's not my ambition; it's God's."

He stared at her. "I beg your pardon?"

She nodded happily. "Isn't it great? It's all his doing. He told me to take care of his lambs, and that's exactly what I'm going to do."

He stared at her, waves of hot and then cold washing over him. "God told you...what?"

"To take care of his lambs. Oh, it's going to be great!" She fixed him with a look that warmed him all the way down to the soles of his boots. "And you're going to help me!"

He nodded, bemused. Of course. It all made perfect sense. Kitty was going to take care of God's lambs, and he was going to take care of Kit—

Wait a minute!

"I'm what?" he said, scowling. "What do you mean I'm going to help you?"

"Of course," she said, taking his arm and tugging him into the dining room, where she had papers spread out all across the table. "God knew I'd need someone I could trust to do this, and that's why he brought you here. To help me."

Jericho shook his head. "Kitty, slow down. What on earth are you talking about?"

She laughed. "I'm sorry, Jericho. I know I'm not making much sense." She took his arm again. "Come take a look at what I've drawn here."

The drawings were actually quite good. She'd sketched the floor plan of her home, showing both floors, and the backyard. He leaned in closer, studying her notations, then turned to looked at her, perplexed.

"You're making your house into a kennel?"

Her expression was full of strength and determination. "Only part of it. I'm putting a dog run in the backyard that will have both a free area and several separate cages." She pointed to the drawings. "I want you to change these upstairs rooms— the den and the two guest rooms. What I'd really like is to knock out the connecting walls—" she broke off and looked up at him. "Is that possible?"

He nodded slowly. "Sure, but—"

"Good. Then we can partition that area so that there are six or seven smaller enclosures, as well as a main area. That way I can use the enclosures for animals who need their own space and the larger area for crates when they're needed."

Jericho felt as though he'd been tossed into a Tilt-a-Whirl. "Kitty, hang on. These changes will take a lot of planning. And money."

She nodded confidently. "I know that. I can handle it. Dan left me quite well off."

"It's going to be a lot of work," he said doubtfully. "Between all these changes inside and out, it could take months to get it all done."

Her radiant grin was a thing of beauty. "Then we'd better

get started, hadn't we? I'll need you to give me a list of supplies—"

"Whoa, slow down there!" Jericho straightened up abruptly. "I've got other jobs lined up already, remember?" He'd made it very clear to her and her son that he couldn't do more work beyond this week.

Her velvety eyes came to rest on his face, a slight frown creasing her brow. He had to fight the urge to reach out and smooth that troubled expression from her features.

Take care of my lamb....

He clenched his jaw and pushed the words—and his feelings—away. *No! No way.*

"That could be a problem," she said thoughtfully.

He gave a snort. "Yes, Kitty, it could." All of it! Doing the work, being around her, caring about her...

She looked at him, crestfallen. A twinge of guilt struck him. *This isn't my problem!* he told himself firmly.

Then why do you feel so rotten? his conscience returned. *Could it be because you know how much she's come to depend on you over the past few weeks, and you haven't done anything to stop it?*

He wanted to deny it, but he couldn't. He'd watched the change in Kitty, the way she'd light up when he got there in the mornings, the effort she put into having coffee waiting for him, fixed just the way he liked. She'd even taken to making him his favorite sandwiches for lunch.

It had been pretty clear that she was coming to look on him as part of her family. And while he'd known it wasn't wise, he hadn't done anything to dispel the image.

Because you liked it. You wanted it. For that matter, you nurtured it. Again, he knew it was the truth. Oh, sure, he'd done his best those first few days to get out of the house as quickly as he could. He'd run, figuratively and almost literally, back to the calm of his nice ordered life. Each day as he went home, he breathed a sigh of relief. So what if his house seemed too quiet. And oddly lacking…something.

Someone, the inner voice supplied, but he ignored it.

He'd been resolute in turning down her end-of-the-day offers of a cup of coffee, and he'd done so without looking too cold. Or too panicked.

Then it happened. Defeat. She'd made hot cider, and the welcoming aroma of cinnamon—and the inviting warmth in her smile and in those tantalizing brown eyes—wore him down. "Just this once," he said, accepting the mug she offered him.

Are you crazy? he yelled at himself. *Get out! Run!*

But he didn't do either. He just followed Kitty to the living room.

And so it had begun. That was the first step in what became an established pattern of sitting and talking with her before he left each afternoon. He wasn't much of a talker, but that hadn't hindered them at all. She did most of the talking, almost as though she'd been cut off from people for months and was suddenly overflowing with the need to share. She told him about her childhood, her husband, and her kids. And as he listened, something terrible happened.

He started to care.

Stupid, stupid! he'd told himself over and over. *Forget her. Get out now!*

As much as he'd pretended otherwise, he knew it was the only thing he could do. It grew clearer every day. He and Kitty were polar opposites. He needed order, harmony, structure, routine, peace, and tranquillity. And Kitty?

Kitty was chaos incarnate.

Wherever she went, pandemonium followed. Oh, sure, it was usually fun pandemonium, but it was pandemonium all the same. She didn't think like he did, talk like he did—nothing about her made sense to his way of thinking.

It was his way of feeling that was giving him trouble. As far as his rebellious heart was concerned, everything about Kitty Hawk made sense.

But nothing was going to happen with them. It couldn't. He was decided. So he'd known this day would come, when he'd have to walk away from this woman who was starting to mean more to him than was good for either of them. The best thing he could do for her, and for himself, was to walk away and forget he'd ever known her.

All he had to do was figure out how to do that without ripping his heart out in the process.

"I know."

He turned startled eyes to her. "What?" Had she reached the point where she could read his thoughts?

"I know what we'll do." The shine was back in her eyes. She reached out to take his hand in hers. "We'll pray about it."

Exasperation filled him. "Kitty, come on! Don't you think the God of the universe has more important things on his mind than my work schedule? Come into reality, will you? I can't—no, I *won't* go crying to God to fix every little detail of my piddly little concerns! I don't work like that. *God* doesn't work like that!"

He turned away from her, quick regret coming on the heels of his heated words. He didn't want to look at her, to see the hurt or disappointment on her face.

"Jericho?"

He turned slowly and met her gaze—then stared at her, puzzled. There wasn't even a hint of disappointment in her eyes. Quite the opposite, her expression was one of…what? Understanding? Compassion? Care? He wasn't sure. Then a gentle smile spread over her features. "It's okay," she said gently. "I'll pray for both of us because I know God will have an answer."

Her faith was so sincere, so…childlike. She was the oddest combination of maturity and innocence he'd ever encountered. He sighed.

"Okay, Kitty. You go ahead and pray. But don't blame me if you're disappointed."

She patted him on the arm as though he were the one who needed comforting. "Relax, Jericho. Everything's going to work out just fine."

Looking into those soft, brown eyes, he smiled. He could almost believe she was right.

That night, Kitty lay in bed, engrossed in her Bible reading. Suddenly she stopped, stared, and read the verse in front of her again.

"Now the gates of Jericho were tightly shut because the people were afraid."

Pray for Jericho.

The urging was strong and undeniable.

Kitty slid from the bed and knelt beside it. God had brought down the walls of Jericho once before. Though this was a different Jericho, and the walls were a different kind of walls, the problem seemed to be the same.

Fear. Her fear of letting go of the past. His fear of…well, she wasn't sure what Jericho was afraid of. But she could tell he was.

So she followed the leading of the still, small voice and

brought the problem to the only place it could be solved: the throne of God.

FIVE

I t was early morning a few days later when Kitty's phone
rang.

She cast a glance at the clock, wondering who would be
calling her so early. "Hello?"

"You win."

"Jericho?"

"Look, if you're going to gloat—"

"No, no," Kitty stopped him. "I wouldn't dream of it." She
frowned. "At least not until you tell me what it is I'm not gloating over."

Silence.

"Jericho?"

"I still don't think God is just sitting there, ready to jump in
and take care of our every little problem. I just want that clear
right up front, okay?"

Sudden excitement bubbled inside of Kitty, but she forced
her tone to stay even. "Okay."

"All right. I got four calls yesterday. From clients."

"And?"

"And they wanted to postpone the work they'd contracted
me to do."

"You're kidding!"

"I don't kid about my work, Kitty."

"Right," she said, grateful he wasn't there to see the grin
spreading over her face. *I knew you'd work it out, Lord!* her heart

sang. "That's true. Should have remembered that. So…?"

"So I've suddenly found myself with several months of open time—"

"You're going to do the work on my place!" She couldn't help the glee that filled her voice.

"You're gloating," he said gloomily.

"I'm sorry. I'll behave." But she blew that promise right out the window with the next breath, "Sooooo, kinda looks like God got involved after all, doesn't it?" She knew she sounded smug, but she didn't care. She was too excited.

"I'm hanging up now," came the disgusted response.

"Okay, okay, I'll be good," she said, laughing.

"That," he said darkly, "will be the day."

"Sourpuss," she shot at him, giving up her struggle to contain her laughter.

"Pollyanna," he retorted with a snort, but she heard the amusement in his voice as well. "See you tomorrow morning. Early."

"I'll be counting the hours." She sounded revoltingly perky, even to her own ears, but she didn't care. God was at work, and she was so excited she could hardly contain herself.

SIX

"You want to what?"

Jericho stared at Kitty in utter disbelief. She couldn't be serious. *This is Kitty*, he reminded himself, studying her expression. *Of course she can.*

"I want to start bringing in clients."

"You mean animals."

"Right. That's what I said."

He looked away, the battle inside raging again. *She's crazy, Lord. I keep telling you that. She's crazy.*

Lean not on your own understanding.

It's the understanding you gave me, he retorted, frustrated. *And it's done just fine for fifty years. It's helped me build a successful business. It's supplied me with a great income and a nice home. Why change now?*

The response came from somewhere in the region of his heart. *It's not good for man to be alone.*

He closed his mind to the truth of the words and shook his head, giving Kitty a stern look. "No way. The work's not done."

His heart sank at the patient—and determined—look in her chocolate eyes.

"Jericho, it's time."

"And you know this *how*, exactly?" he challenged, knowing even as he said it what the answer would be.

"It's just a feeling."

Bingo.

"But it's a very clear feeling."

Oh, of course.

"God's ready for me to get started, Jericho. And I need to do so."

He wasn't going to win. He could see that. "Just the upstairs," he said gloomily. "I'm nearly done up there. A few vent covers, some trim, a few touches of paint, and I'm done."

The warmth of her smile echoed in her voice. "Thank you."

"But you keep the critters quiet and under control, understood?"

She met his stern gaze with a look of wide-eyed innocence. "Of course."

"Okay, team, progress report."

Brendan and Kylie grinned at their grandfather.

"Everything's going great, sir," Kylie said happily. "It's been weeks since the operation was implemented, and Mom not only still has Bosco but she just called me to say she thinks she'll keep him. What's more, she's really moving forward with this new business of hers." She beamed happily.

"Has she actually started sitting for any pets?" Grams asked with interest.

Kylie laughed. "The whole upstairs is full of critters," she said. "As soon as people found out about her, she had more calls than she could handle. At last count she had two kittens, a little dog, four ferrets, not counting Bosco, and the cat from hell."

"Excuse me?" Grams broke in.

Kylie grinned. "No joke. This cat is huge. He's got to weigh in at thirty pounds, and every ounce is pure orneriness. His name is Godfrey, but Jericho calls him Godzilla."

"Speaking of our Mr. Jericho…Brendan?" Gramps asked.

"Let's just say I think Mom will be keeping more than just the ferret," Brendan responded with a cheeky grin.

"Your repairman?"

"No," Brendan said, chuckling. "At this point, I'd say Jericho Katz has definitely become Mom's repairman."

"Even better," Gramps said, a satisfied smile on his face. "Even better."

"Outta my way!" Kitty screeched as she made a dive for the door. She slid through and slammed it shut behind her. The thud of something solid slamming into the door was followed by a sound that resembled a mix between a wailing banshee and an out-of-control set of bagpipes.

"I take it Godzilla didn't care for his din-din?"

She looked toward the stairs, where Jericho stood leaning against the wall with a grin on his face.

"*Godfrey*," she corrected through gritted teeth, "won't care for din-din until it's me."

Shaking her head, she came to walk down the stairs with Jericho. She should have been tipped off that Godfrey was not going to be an easy job when his owners called and begged her to watch the cat for them while they went on vacation for a week. The desperation in their voices should have clued her in. But she'd been so excited when Jericho told her she could use the upstairs, and even more excited to have her second pet-sitting client, that she'd agreed without question.

Her first client, of course, had been Sweetums. Kitty had no

70

sooner gotten the go-ahead from Jericho than she was on the phone.

"Miss Lily?" she said. "How would you like to go visit your daughter?"

Sweetums was, even now, happily situated upstairs.

If only Godfrey were so easy to care for! His owners had requested that she pick the cat up at their apartment, explaining that a neighbor would let her in and that Godfrey's carrying case would be on the kitchen counter. When she arrived at their apartment, the neighbor threw the door open, then slammed it shut behind Kitty, muttering something about crazy women who took their lives into their own hands.

Despite all these clues, it wasn't until Kitty had gone into the bedroom, where the owners had told her to look, that she knew she was in trouble. The cat was under the bed, surrounded by dust bunnies. And when Kitty tried the age-old, "Here, kitty, kitty," he met her with a malevolent glare and a snarling hiss deep in his throat.

She wondered if it would be good enough to take the dust bunnies home.

"Listen, cat," she said after half an hour of ineffectual coaxing, "I'm smarter than you are." She met Godfrey's evil gaze and swallowed. "I hope."

She found his plastic food dish, filled it with food in the hopes of making friends, and slid it toward the beast. The hiss turned to a screech, and Kitty beat a hasty retreat. She'd come back twenty minutes later, knelt down, and found the shredded remains of the food dish.

Of course, all the food was gone. Godfrey obviously didn't miss a meal if he could avoid it.

It had taken a call to Kylie for help, and thanks to a dose of tranquilizer placed in the cat's food in a new metal dish, Kitty was able to pry him from his hiding place. Dragging the unconscious, oversized creature out from under the bed was a task. So was getting him into his carrier.

Fortunately, Jericho was there when she came home and carried the massive cat up to his room.

There, she thought, pleased, as she settled him in his sectioned-off sleeping area. *Welcome to your vacation home.*

But when the cat awoke, it went berserk. Its bloodcurdling yowl and whirling-dervish reaction reminded Kitty of the Tasmanian devil on Saturday morning cartoons. Maddened creature at her heels, Kitty had scrambled up on top of her dresser, barely managing to evade the cat as he flew by her, claws flailing, out the door of the room.

Before she could react, he'd barreled into her bedroom and ensconced himself under her bed. Kitty slammed that door shut and waited for Jericho to come the next morning to check things out.

Together they opened the door, only to discover total mayhem. Her curtains were shredded, the lamp was on the floor, her books were scattered across the bed, and the pillows were decimated.

"Oh no," she groaned. Jericho did his best to restrain his laughter, but had little success.

"You're never going to get him out of here," he said.

With a boldness born of frustration, she marched into the cat's territory, grabbed her Bible and a blanket, and marched back out the door. "Not a problem," she said with confidence. "The couch is more comfortable than my bed."

That was three days ago, and she'd been sleeping on the couch ever since.

"At least the others aren't hard to take care of," she said with relief as they reached the bottom of the stairs, and Jericho glanced at her.

"Yet."

Later that day Kitty went up to check on the ferrets. She'd situated the four little scamps in one of the "stalls," as Jericho called them, in what was now the community room. She surveyed the room with satisfaction.

Jericho had done a great job. The connecting walls had been removed, and the room now consisted of ten stalls with latching doors, one large open area for crates, and another large area for play time.

At one end of the room, Sweetums was happily snoozing. Two stalls down from her were Tango and Cash, two cuddly little kittens. The ferrets were at the far end of the room.

After her escapades with Bosco, Kitty hadn't been sure how she'd do with four of the little mischief makers at once, but so far they'd been little furry angels—despite Jericho's dire warnings. He'd spent half an hour trying to talk Kitty into setting up a cage for the four.

"Their owner said he usually keeps them in a cage."

"Unless he's home," she argued. "They'll be fine."

"Bosco wouldn't be fine," Jericho countered with a snort.

"Bosco is an aberration of nature," Kitty retorted. "I can't believe all ferrets are so predisposed to mischief making."

She'd given them towels for curling in and an assortment of toys. The ferrets seemed thrilled. They played together, wrestling and tussling until they tired themselves out. They were all trained to a litter pan, so cleanup was minimal. All

Kitty had to do was refill their water and food dishes and play with them a couple of times a day.

She'd come up with a great idea for a bed for them, too: a beanbag chair. "They'll love the thing," she told the still-doubting Jericho. And she was right. When they'd completely exhausted themselves, they curled up together in the middle of the bag and went to sleep.

All her clients should be so compliant.

Still smiling, she opened the door to the ferrets' stall—and froze.

"Jericho!" she wailed, staring in dismay at the disorder before her. The beloved bean bag was nearly flat. Kitty could see holes in the cloth where the ferrets had apparently chewed through. The foam-bead filling was spread everywhere, covering the floor and adhering to the walls thanks to static electricity.

She heard footsteps come pounding up the stairs, and a wide-eyed Jericho rushed into the room.

"What?"

"Look," she wailed, and he came to survey the damage.

His gaze came back to hers. "The ferrets?"

She shrugged, scanning the mess for some sign of life. "I don't know, but they couldn't have gotten out, could they?"

He looked at her sideways. "They're ferrets."

Kitty's heart fell. He was right.

Suddenly a chorus of chirps and little grunts sounded, and Kitty looked to find two little foam-bead-covered ferret heads popping out of the decimated beanbag.

Even their twitching whiskers had beads on them!

But they were safe. And that was what really mattered.

Jericho shifted beside her, and she turned to him, holding up a hand to forestall the "I told you so" that she knew she deserved. Their eyes met.

"You were right," she said quietly.

He clamped his mouth shut, nodded, then headed for the door. "I'll set up the cage as soon as you get the mess cleaned up."

At least he had the grace to sound only a little smug.

SEVEN

What now? Jericho wondered from his perch atop a ladder when the doorbell pealed for the umpteenth time.

"Can you get that?" Kitty called from upstairs. "I'm giving Sweetums a bath."

"Of course you are," Jericho mumbled, coming down the ladder and heading for the door. "I'm a repairman!" he yelled as he pulled the door open. "*Not* a receptionis—"

The word froze on his lips. He stared, then went to the bottom of the stairs. "Kitty, there's some clown at the door for you."

She appeared at the top of the stairs, a soggy, suds-covered Sweetums cradled in her hands. "There's no need to be rude," she scolded.

He shook his head, pointing to the front door. "I'm not."

She came down the stairs, then paused, gawking at the fully decked-out circus clown—complete with red nose, big shoes, and a bouquet of balloons—standing on her doorstep.

Jericho shrugged. Only at Kitty's house.

He walked back toward the living room and the relative safety of his ladder when sudden chaos in the form of barking and growling and a frantic bellow spun him back around.

The clown was now inside the house and waving his arms frantically, which made the balloons attached to one wrist dance and bounce against the ceiling. He held one leg out and shook it furiously.

At the end of that leg, attached to the clown's big floppy shoe, was a snarling Sweetums. The usually docile animal had become a ten-pound bundle of suds-covered fury.

"Get this oversized *rat* off my shoe!" the clown yelped.

"Rat?" Kitty echoed. "Sweetums is nothing of the kind! I'll have you know she's from the purest line of—"

"Lady, do I look like I *care*?" the clown yelled.

Jericho started to run toward the melee, but Kitty put her hand out to stop him. "Wait! Grab the stuffed sock!" she said in a surprisingly unruffled voice.

He stared at her. As amazed by her calm as her words. "What?"

"The stuffed sock. On the couch."

Without asking for an explanation, he went to do as she bid. Sure enough, a stuffed sock was there. He grabbed it and tossed it to Kitty.

She turned to the clown and said, "Sir, stop trying to pull away."

"Are you nuts? He'll eat me alive!"

She fixed the clown with a firm, commanding look. "Sir! The dog isn't big enough to eat you alive. Your shoe will protect you for the few seconds it takes me to distract her, but you have to stop fighting her." Kitty narrowed her eyes, watching the terrier's determined assault. "*Now*, sir. Unless, of course, you *want* her crawling up your leg?"

The clown froze and let his leg drop, which brought Sweetums's feet in contact with the floor. Kitty pounced on the opportunity to wave the sock in front of the terrier's little nose.

"Hey, Sweetums! Get the sock!"

The dog launched herself at the sock, latching onto it with abandon. Kitty lifted the sock, Sweetums and all, into her arms. The little dog chewed and shook the sock, seemingly content.

Jericho stared at Kitty in amazement, and she grinned at him. "I'll be right back. Why don't you see if our friend here was hurt."

Within minutes, she was back, still smiling that unruffled smile. "Now, then," she said to the clown, who was now sitting on the stairs. "What can I do for you?"

The clown paused, drew a deep breath as though to compose himself, then stood up and said in a voice that would have done Sylvester the cat proud: "*Thay* there! Would you be the famouth Kitty Hawk?"

Jericho leaned against the couch, ready to enjoy the show. Kitty didn't disappoint him. With a laugh, she replied in a lisping voice, "Thufferin' thuccotash! Thath me."

Now it was the clown's turn to stare. "Look, lady," he said in a tone that was clear evidence he'd reached the end of his rope. "I just got attacked by a rat with a thyroid problem, my once size-eleven foot is now probably a size eight, and I'm running a half-hour behind. On top of all of that, I get to do a birthday party today for forty sugar-crazed ten-year-olds. So, please, do you think you could do me the monumental favor of not stepping on my lines?"

Jericho stepped forward, suddenly protective. "Listen, buddy," he said, "there's no reason to talk to the lady that way."

The clown backpedaled quickly, but Kitty put a restraining hand on Jericho's arm. He reached up to cover it with his own, looking down into her smiling face.

"Thanks," she said softly, then turned to the clown. "I apologize. Please, the floor is all yours."

With that, the colorful character began dancing around and

honking his horn, singing off-key, "Let me call you *Thwee*theart, I've a gift for yoooooouuu...."

At the end of the song, he held out the balloons with a flourish and handed them to her. "Happy April Fools', one day early," he said. "From Brendan and Kylie."

"Um, thanks," Kitty said, her lips twitching. "You were great."

The clown didn't reply. But as he turned to leave, Jericho heard him mutter all the way to the door, "Be a clown, they said. Make people laugh. Fill your days with fun." He pulled the door open with a snort. "Who were they kidding?"

"Do you want to tell him, or shall I?" Jericho asked Kitty, and she tilted her head curiously. "You don't have to be a clown for those things." He grinned. "All you have to do is hang around with Kitty Hawk."

She laughed, her cheeks becoming a shade of pink. "Lan' sakes, Mistuh Katz," she said in a fine southern accent as she turned to go back up the stairs, balloons in tow. "You just gonna make my head spin with such fine praise."

Frankly, my dear, Jericho thought ruefully as he headed back to his ladder. *I do give a darn. Far more than I should.*

"Thanks for the balloons; they were great."

Kylie and Brendan smiled at Kitty. The three of them were out to dinner together.

"Glad you liked them, Mom," Kylie said. "They reminded us of you."

"And of Dad," Brendan added.

Kitty smiled. She could think of Dan now without so much pain. "Me, too."

"So, Mom," Brendan said, "how's Mr. Katz?"

She met her son's gaze and noted the humor twinkling in his eyes. "Fine."

"How are you two getting along?"

"Brendan!" Kylie punched his arm, but Kitty just laughed.

"I think we're getting along pretty well," she said, watching her children's faces carefully. "In fact, I'd say very well."

To Kitty's relief, Kylie and Brendan looked pleased.

"So you don't mind?" she asked. "If I like Jericho?"

"We're glad, Mom," Kylie answered softly. "We want you to be happy again."

Brendan looked suddenly serious. "There's just one thing you need to be sure of, Mom."

"What do you mean?"

A grin broke across his face. "Well, if you and Jericho end up being really serious about each other..." he paused, and Kitty considered him curiously.

"Then?"

Kylie laughed suddenly. "Oh, my, I never even thought about that."

"Brendan, what do I need to be sure of?" Kitty asked, confused.

Brendan's smile was full of delight. "That you don't mind going from Kitty Hawk—"

"To Kitty Katz!" Kylie finished with a giggle. "Proof positive, Mom. This is a match made in heaven!"

"It could be," Kitty agreed. "But first we've got some walls to demolish."

Brendan stared at her. "I thought the walls were down."

"Not quite," Kitty said with a confident smile. "But God and I are working on it."

~ ~ ~ ~ ~

Jericho dropped his bag of groceries on the table in his kitchen and flipped on the light.

He stood still for a moment, savoring the silence. No animals grunting or barking or meowing. No phones ringing off the hook. No people coming to pick up their furry or feathered babies. No Kitty yelling for him when the next disaster strikes.

Just peace and quiet. *Pure heaven,* he told himself. Yup, that was the way he liked it. Quiet. Silent. Really silent.

He glanced around.

Too silent.

"Yeah, well," he said gloomily, "you'd better get used to it, bucko. You refused to get attached, so don't be complaining now that it's over." And over it was. He had one more day of work left at Kitty's house. That was it. He sat down in a chair and stared bleakly at the calendar on the wall.

Tomorrow was April Fools' day.

He shook his head. What a fitting day to say good-bye to a dream he could not quite believe in.

EIGHT

R owf! Rrrrrowf! Yap! Yap!"

"Kitty!"

"*Bark! Bark-bark-bark! Yap!*"

Jericho slammed down his hammer and stalked to the bottom of the stairs. The day had been frustrating enough without having to listen to Sweetums.

Jericho had tried a dozen times to tell Kitty today was his last day. But every time he tried, the words stuck in his throat. And one phrase repeated itself over and over in his mind....

Tend my lamb.

He'd done everything he could to get it out of his head, but there was no stopping it.

So, okay. He might not be able to still the voice within. But he could sure do something about that darned dog! "Kitty!"

"I'm right here. You don't have to yell."

He jumped and spun around. She was standing right behind him. Close behind him. Too close.

Her warm breath fanned his face as she asked, "Did you want to say something?"

Startled by her sudden proximity, he took a quick step backward. Unfortunately, the stairs were in his way. He hit the stair with the back of his foot and went flying.

"Look out!" Kitty grabbed at him in a frantic effort to keep him from falling, but she only succeeded in being thrown off balance herself by his momentum. They both landed with a thud, Jericho on the stairs, Kitty on his chest.

He lay there, groaning, uncertain what hurt more: his back, upon which, from top to bottom, the stairs were now imprinted—or his heart, where in some inexorable, impossible way, this woman was now imprinted.

A soft hand came to touch his face gently. "Are you all right?"

He closed his eyes, savoring her nearness, telling himself to get up and yet feeling unable to comply.

"Bark! Yap-yap-yap! Bark! Rrrrrowf!"

His eyes flew open, and he shifted to a sitting position, then helped Kitty to her feet. "What is wrong with that dog?"

Kitty patted him on the arm consolingly. "Sweetums must be missing Miss Lily," she said. "I'll see if I can find her rubber bone."

"When you do," Jericho grumbled as she went up the stairs, "try stuffing it in her mouth."

Kitty entered the animal room and grimaced. The little dog's sharp bark was piercing. It was enough to make your ears bleed.

Looking around, Kitty spotted the terrier standing near the heating vent, barking at it furiously.

"Sweetums, what's wrong, little girl?"

The dog didn't even look at her. Coming closer, Kitty saw that the vent cover was missing. She went to pick Sweetums up and cuddle her comfortingly, but Sweetums bolted from her arms and went back to barking at the open vent. "Sweetums, this has got to stop!"

Kitty looked around the room for the silky's rubber bone. Miss Lily had been very clear: Sweetums *loved* that bone. She carried it everywhere, slept with it, took it outside when she did her "business," kept it near her dish while she ate. If anything could mollify the little dog, it would be the bone.

But it was nowhere in sight.

"Kitty, for cryin' out loud," Jericho came in the door. "Shut that walking dustmop up!"

"I would if I could," she said calmly. "Come in here, and help me find her bone."

"Oh, for the love of—" he broke off, then shook his head. "Fine. Whatever it takes."

Together they tore the room apart. No bone. Dismayed, Kitty looked at Jericho. "I can't believe it's gone," she said. "What could have hap—"

She broke off when Jericho put his hand on her arm, looking toward the offending floor vent.

Kitty's eyes widened in understanding. "No! You don't mean...?"

Jericho nodded. "The bone's in the vent. It's the only thing that makes sense." He headed for the door, muttering, "I don't believe this. I simply don't believe it."

Kitty scooped Sweetums up, grabbed her leash, and caught up with Jericho. "Will it be hard to find?"

He turned and fixed her with a glare.

"Okay, okay," she said quickly, "we'll go for a walk. Will half an hour do?"

No response.

"Right. We'll be back in an hour."

I love her.

The unspoken admission resounded in Jericho's mind and heart as he walked around the house to the crawl-space door.

Father God, I love her. She's crazy, irrational, a complete dreamer...and I can't fathom living another day without her.

He pulled the cover aside and went down on his belly, crawling under the house, through the dirt and grime and spiderwebs. When he spotted the ductwork, he rolled over and stared at it as images drifted through his mind....

Kitty the way he'd first seen her, covered with little white flour pawprints where Bosco had run across her as he raced for freedom....

Kitty's sweet face, flushed with chagrin when she found the ferrets had trashed the beanbag....

Kitty leaning against the door, laughing ruefully after a narrow escape from Godzilla....

Kitty's warm brown eyes studying him over a cup of coffee.... Kitty's hand, warm on his arm....

He reached up to cut through the ductwork carefully.

She's the most amazing woman I've ever met, he thought.

He shook his head. He hadn't thought it possible. He'd been so sure when Alice died that he'd never fall in love again. After all, he'd never find another Alice. And that was true. Kitty was nothing like his first wife.

And yet...her perpetual merriment touched him deeply. The myriad expressions that played across her features intrigued him, and he found himself ridiculously preoccupied with trying to discern what she was thinking and feeling.

Her mere presence brought him joy. It was just that simple.

Tell her.

The ductwork came free, and he reached inside, feeling carefully. "Gotcha!" he chortled as his fingers closed around a hard rubber item. He pulled it out and stared at it, then nodded.

"Okay, Lord, you win," he said. "I'll tell her. Just do me a favor and help her see she definitely needs me." He laid his head back in the dirt. "Almost as much as I need her."

NINE

An hour later, Kitty brought a still-frantic Sweetums home. The dog's energy was astounding. She'd loved the walk, and she'd told Kitty so as vocally as possible.

Kitty reached down to scoop her up and place her hand loosely on her muzzle. "Shhhhh!" she scolded as she opened the door. "Jericho will have your furry little head if you don't shut up."

"I may do that in any case," a low voice growled.

Kitty started at the sight that greeted her. Jericho was covered in dirt and grime from head to toe. "What happened to you?" she exclaimed.

"I met you," he replied gloomily.

"Ha ha," she retorted.

"You think I'm kidding?"

"Never mind," she said, coming in and standing a safe distance away. "Did you find the bone?"

He held out something as dirty and grimy as he was. Sweetums barked ecstatically, jumped from Kitty's arms, and ran to jump up on Jericho's legs.

"Can you say 'drop kick,' Sweetums?" he asked.

"Don't you dare!" Kitty came forward to pluck the disgusting bone from his fingers and drop it down to Sweetums.

"No! Wait!" Jericho said frantically, but it was too late. Sweetums, bone firmly in her mouth, made a mad dash for the stairs.

"Stop her!" Jericho bellowed, and Kitty scrambled to obey. But the little dog dodged her skillfully, standing at the top of the stairs and watching her race after her, Jericho right behind her, as though to say, "Hey! Chase! Cool!"

"Come back here, you little—"

"Jericho! If you sound angry she won't come!" Kitty scolded.

Sure enough, at their exchange, Sweetums spun and bolted for her room.

"Stop her!" Jericho yelled again.

Together they bounded up the stairs and ran to the room, entering just in time to see Sweetums standing at the edge of the still-uncovered vent. She looked up at them just long enough to be sure she had an audience, then turned and dropped the bone down the hole.

Kitty and Jericho stared at the now happily yapping terrier and listened to the bone bounce its way to the depths of the heating ductwork again.

Kitty bit her lip, afraid to even look at Jericho.

His laughter, deep and rich, suddenly filled the room. She looked up at him in amazement. He was leaning against the doorjamb, laughing so hard now that he was holding his sides, and tears were running down his face, leaving trails in the dirt.

Kitty's sense of humor took over, and she laughed in answer to his unrestrained mirth. He held a hand out to her, and she took it, letting him pull her into the circle of his arms.

He cradled her gently against his chest, looking down at her with so much tenderness that her heart skipped a beat. Gently he cupped her face in his hands, then, as though it was the most natural thing in the world, he leaned down to press a soft kiss against her lips.

"I love you," he said when he lifted his head.

"This isn't an April Fools' joke, is it?" she demanded, almost afraid to believe what she was hearing.

He laughed. "The only joke was my thinking I could walk away from you, Kitty. I know now that's something I don't want to do."

She smiled at him, reaching up to touch his face. "The walls have come crashing down, haven't they?"

He didn't even ask her what she meant. She could see in his eyes that he knew. "Absolutely. I did everything I could to keep them in place, but God showed me, through you, and that crazy little dog, and all these days of the most wonderful chaos I've ever known, that this is for real. I'm well and truly in love with you. And I'm going to marry you. So you may as well accept that fact. We belong together, Kitty. Now—" he caressed her face—"and, God willing, for all our days."

"Oh. That's nice," she breathed, joy filling her. "Because I love you, too. And I don't even mind."

"Mind?" he asked, his eyes twinkling with humor.

"That you'll be making my name more outrageous than it's ever been."

She felt his chuckle deep in his chest. "It's only fair. Considering what you'll be doing to my nice, ordered life." He kissed her again, and it was as though light and laughter and joy surrounded them. Her heart sang out with gratitude to God for all he'd given her, all he'd taught her, and all the blessings the future so clearly held.

"Happy April Fools'," she said to him when she could finally catch her breath.

"The happiest," he replied.

EPILOGUE

"Your mother is a lovely summer bride!"

Kylie and Brendan glanced at the small elderly woman in front of them. Smiles broke out on their faces when they saw the little dog cradled in one arm.

"She certainly is," Kylie said happily, taking the small gloved hand being held out to her. "I'm so glad you and Sweetums could come, Miss Lily. Mom said it wouldn't be the same without you."

"It's just delightful that she chose to have her wedding in the park. Sweetums would have hated to miss this auspicious occasion." The woman's sweet face was wreathed in smiles as she looked to where Kitty and Jericho stood together. "I must say, Kitty and her new beau look so happy together."

"They do, indeed," Brendan agreed, a slightly smug note in his voice.

"How good of God to bring them together," Miss Lily said. She patted their hands and then moved away, holding a piece of wedding cake out for Sweetums to nibble on as she walked.

"Touché," Brendan said with a small smile. "Put in my place by a woman who talks to her dog."

Kylie laughed. "If I'm half so elegant and sweet when I'm older, I'll be thrilled."

"Congratulations, team." A voice came from behind them, and they turned to grin at their grandfather. He was holding three plastic goblets of punch. "A toast," he quipped as they each took a glass.

"To us," Brendan said, lifting his glass high.

"To Mom and Jericho," Kylie added.

"To a mission well accomplished," Gramps finished.

They clinked the goblets together, then drained them.

"Pity there's no fireplace to cast them into," Brendan said.

"Not necessary." Gramps took the empty goblets. "I'll just put these away in case I need them again."

"Need them again?" Kylie asked. "For what?"

"Never can tell," Gramps said, "when the need will arise to celebrate another successful operation."

"Gramps, Mom's doing great. She's not going to need us again," Brendan pointed out.

"True," the older man replied, a serene smile on his weathered face as he moved away. "But there are others who may yet need some help."

"Others?" Kylie asked.

"People who aren't settled yet, who are wrapped up in their jobs, who need to find as much happiness as your mother has found."

His words drifted back to them as he walked away, and Brendan laughed. "I pity the poor fools, whoever they are."

Kylie grinned, shaking her head sympathetically. "You know Gramps. He won't give up on them until they're 'settled.'"

Brendan looked at her. "Who do we know that's wrapped up in their jobs?"

"No one," Kylie said, watching Gramps. He was deep in conversation with her mom and Jericho. All three were glancing at her and Brendan with secret smiles on their faces. "That is, other than you and m—"

The words died on her lips, and the siblings exchanged suddenly alarmed glances.

"Bren!" Kylie yelped, grabbing her brother's arm. "He wouldn't!"

They spun to look at Gramps. "Oh, no," Brendan groaned.

With that, the two broke into a run, knowing even as they did so that it was too late. Gramps was standing there, talking with Mom and Jericho....They were laughing and smiling secret smiles....

Yup, the signs were all too clear.

Operation Save the Kids had already been activated.

CAT IN THE PIANO

JENNIFER BROOKS

To my sisters and brothers:
Becky, Jeff, Rachel, Steve, and Hazel.
With thanks for your love, support, and
willing research assistance.

ONE

C aleb Murphy double-checked the paper in his hand to make sure he had the right address, then looked back up at the old San Francisco Victorian. Set in the middle of Pacific Heights, 854 Alder was the strangest looking house he'd ever seen. The shingles and wide front door were the color of grape juice, but the siding was dark green and the porch trim ivory. Twin gables in a shockingly bright yellow stuck out on either end like fat crayons. The brick walk was lined with a riotous mixture of flowers: roses, marigolds, pansies, lilies, snapdragons, and several others he couldn't put a name to. The wrought-iron fence that surrounded the yard was topped every few feet by a cat-shaped ornament.

What was that saying? Poor people are crazy, but rich people are eccentric.

Caleb got out of his car and walked up the front steps. The front porch wrapped around the side of the house, and a swing, painted a brilliant magenta, hung next to the door. On the door, a heavy brass knocker in the shape of a cow stared rather foolishly at Caleb. He chuckled and shook his head. If the house had been like this during Dr. Powell's lifetime, he must have had a quirky sense of humor Caleb hadn't known was there. Caleb lifted the ring that pierced the cow's nose and let it fall. The clang was deafening.

Just as he was about to knock again, the door swung open. The first thing Caleb saw was a large black cat, its golden eyes fixed unblinkingly on his. He had never particularly liked or disliked cats and had always considered them to be like most other animals. Not this cat. Its eyes held more intelligence and personality than most people's. In all his not-quite-thirty years, Caleb had never met another cat like it. He could have sworn the feline was reading his every thought.

Feeling ridiculously self-conscious, he lowered his gaze to the woman whose shoulders supported the cat. She was probably no taller than five feet, with frizzy white hair and sharp black eyes.

"Don't let Vincent scare you. He's really very friendly, but he likes to test people first." The black eyes twinkled.

"Vincent?"

"For Van Gogh, of course. Edward always said they had the same eyes. Edward's grandfather knew him, you know." After tugging Caleb inside, she swung the door closed without disturbing the cat in the least.

"Who?"

"Why, Van Gogh, of course."

Caleb knew he had missed something, but he wasn't going to try to piece her logic together. "Are you Mrs. Dorcas Powell? Dr. Edward Powell's wife? Er, that is—"

"Yes, dear Edward was my husband. For sixty-three wonderful years." She took a tissue from her sleeve and dabbed at the tip of her nose. "I miss him so."

Caleb looked away, uncomfortable. He never knew what to say to people who had suffered a loss. He glanced around. The foyer was enormous, with a great curving staircase of some dark polished wood rising along one side. The floor was tiled in muted green marble, and a crystal teardrop chandelier hovered above his head. He caught a glimpse of his own reflection in a mirrored hat rack and ran one hand through his dark brown hair.

He could hear someone playing the piano in a room off to the right. It was something he'd heard before. Beethoven, maybe? He could never keep all those classical composers straight.

Mrs. Powell took him by the arm and led him across the floor and through an open doorway straight ahead. They entered a formal dining room. A gleaming mahogany table was set with three places. A silver tea service sat on the sideboard. The china and the tea set were the kind Caleb assumed cost an arm and a leg. He'd always thought that if anyone actually bought the stuff, it was only for display. This wasn't even a holiday.

"I'm sorry, Mrs. Powell—"

"Please, call me Dorcas."

Caleb looked down uncomfortably. "Dorcas, I didn't realize you were having guests for dinner. Would you like me to make an appointment to come back another time?"

"Certainly not, Caleb." She wrinkled her nose at him. "You are Caleb Murphy, aren't you?"

"Well, yes."

"Caleb, I wouldn't trust my Edward's book collection to just anyone, you know." She petted Vincent absently. "Before I let you take his books away, I simply must get to know you first."

"But if you have company—"

"My dear, you are my company."

"But there are three places."

"The third is for my granddaughter, of course. Do you think she should eat in the music room by herself?"

"No, I didn't mean—"

"She would do that sometimes if I didn't force her to come out for meals. She gets so wrapped up in her music. Just like Edward. Although Edward couldn't play a note. He did like his medical books, though. He used to sit for hours in his library, right next to the fire, with a dusty old book in his lap. And he was forever losing his spectacles, so he'd have to keep the book about an inch from his nose. Because he got cold easily, he'd sit with his feet practically in the fireplace, and hunched over his books. That is, until they caught on fire."

Caleb felt his heart stop. "The books?"

"No, his pants." She patted Caleb's arm comfortingly. "Oh, don't worry. It only happened once or twice, and that was because the logs fell and shot out sparks. No harm done."

Caleb felt guilty because he'd been so worried about the books catching fire that he hadn't even considered the old man's well-being. But before he could utter a word of apology, he was being pushed into a chair.

"Would you like some tea?" She waved vaguely toward the teapot on the sideboard. "I'll go check on dinner. Vincent always comes with me, of course, but here comes Auguste. He'll keep you company." With that, Dorcas disappeared through a doorway.

Somehow, Caleb wasn't the least surprised to feel a cat rub against his leg. He pushed aside the lace runner on the table and glanced down to see an orange cat, even larger than Vincent. "Let me think," he said, looking into the animal's green eyes. "Who would you be named after?"

"Auguste Rodin."

For an instant, Caleb thought the cat had spoken. But then, he thought absurdly, the cat was a male, and the voice was female. He looked up and into another pair of eyes. These were blue, a startling aquamarine blue, and much more fascinating than any feline eyes.

They belonged to a woman not much taller than Dorcas. She was probably in her late twenties, he guessed, and had the most fascinating, long black curly hair he'd ever seen. It flowed over her arms and reached nearly to her waist. Her skin was very pale and her build small, but her hands—they were the most beautiful hands he'd ever seen in his life. They were narrow and white, with slim, tapering fingers that were surely too long for the rest of her body. And yet they were perfect.

He looked back up to her face and realized she was looking at him as intently as he was looking at her. Abruptly, Auguste moved faster than looked possible for his weight and leaped into the woman's arms. With a chuckle, she caught him.

"Hello. I'm Isobel. Isobel Crawford. Dorcas is my grandmother." Auguste tried to climb around her neck, but she gave him an admonishing look, and he settled back down. "And you must be Caleb Murphy. Dorcas has been talking about you for days."

Caleb nodded. "Yes." He nodded again. "Um, interesting house you have."

"Oh, it's not mine. That is, I've lived here all my life, but I certainly don't think of it as mine. It's Dorcas's."

At that moment, Dorcas came in, bearing an enormous silver soup tureen that looked nearly as big as she. Vincent followed closely behind her, his nose twitching and held high in the air. Caleb couldn't blame him. The scent drifting from that tureen was absolutely heavenly. Caleb moved to take the tureen from her, and she allowed him after a brief struggle.

"Set it there," Dorcas said, nodding toward a spot near the head of the table. Then she turned to her granddaughter.

"Don't be silly, Isobel. This is your house. Perhaps not legally yet, but when I die, all the papers will be in your name. And that won't be long now." She pivoted and returned to the kitchen.

Caleb wasn't sure what to do. He appeared to be in the middle of some family ordeal, and he had no idea how he'd gotten there. Worse, he didn't know how to get uninvolved, since he wasn't used to families. He'd only ever met his mother once, and although he'd lived with his father for the first eighteen years of his life, he could claim he knew his landlady, Mrs. Schmidt, better than he knew his father. And Mrs. Schmidt wasn't particularly chatty.

He turned to Isobel with an apologetic look.

She appeared irritated, but Caleb didn't know why any more than he knew what was going on. He still wasn't quite sure how he'd gotten talked into staying for dinner.

"I'm sure you didn't know what you were getting into when you came here," Isobel said.

Caleb shook his head, speechless.

"Enough of that talk." Dorcas returned, this time laden with a silver tray supporting three plates of salad and a basket of rolls. "This young man must be starving, and we're standing around chatting."

Without further ado, they were all seated at the table, Dorcas at the head and Caleb and Isobel close on either side of her. Dorcas announced that she would ask the blessing.

"Lord, we ask you to bless this food and these two young people with me and what they have ahead of them tonight, in Jesus' name. Amen."

Caleb wondered if he'd heard her correctly. Surely she hadn't meant what he and *Isobel* would do tonight; he was here to talk to Dorcas. But he didn't have time to dwell on the thought.

"Soup?"

Caleb looked up just in time to receive the bowl thrust at him. It was a fragrant and creamy shrimp bisque, garnished with whole shrimp around the edge of the bowl. He ate every drop and barely restrained himself from licking the bowl clean. Then came the warm, crusty rolls and a salad of asparagus and tomatoes topped with a sesame vinaigrette.

"Oh, how rude of me!" Dorcas said suddenly. She looked at Caleb with a gleam in her eyes. "Do you need to call your wife to let her know you won't be home for dinner?"

He shook his head. "I'm not married."

"I see." Dorcas smiled.

Several times Caleb tried to start a conversation about the books, which were after all the purpose of his visit, but Dorcas stopped him, finally saying bluntly, "Don't ruin your digestion with business talk. Wait until after dinner."

They chatted a bit about the house, which, it turned out, had been painted just last month, and then Dorcas asked Isobel about her music lessons that day. Caleb was told that Isobel taught private piano lessons twenty hours a week, and "Oh," said Dorcas, rolling her eyes, "Isobel has the most trying time with those Plunkett twins." She winked. "The way they play sounds just like their name."

The conversation was punctuated with noise from the two cats, who were going wild over the seafood smells. Caleb thought he saw Isobel passing bits of shrimp to Auguste, but he couldn't be sure. Dorcas was more obvious; when she got up to take away the soup bowls and salad plates, she tossed a couple of shrimp tails onto the floor, which the cats immediately snatched and carried under the table. A crunching sound followed.

Over the main course of paella—a hearty stew of seafood,

chicken, sausage, and rice—Dorcas looked up and held Caleb's gaze with her piercing black eyes. "So, Caleb, are you dating anyone?"

At that moment, a mussel lodged itself in Caleb's throat, making him unable to breathe, let alone speak. After a fit of coughing, several gulps of water, and several enthusiastic whacks between the shoulder blades, administered by Dorcas, Caleb recovered. Thankfully Dorcas seemed to have forgotten her question, and the rest of the course was consumed in silence.

Caleb wasn't sure he'd ever need to eat again after finishing his paella, but Dorcas popped up once more to bring in dessert, and he groaned.

"Almond-macaroon tart," said Dorcas. "Isobel made it herself. She does wonderful things with pastry."

Caleb told Isobel he was sure it would be delicious, but when he actually took a bite, he thought he'd died and passed into the hereafter. The mixture of chocolate, coconut, and almonds was incredible. He couldn't help the sigh of pure pleasure that escaped him.

"Isobel will make some man a very lucky husband someday," Dorcas said. "You know what they say about the way to a man's heart."

Since he was starting to get used to her comments, Caleb didn't choke this time. He merely looked at Isobel and said evenly, "I'm sure she will."

Isobel met his gaze and smiled with a mixture of embarrassment and apology, as if she'd heard her grandmother use that line more than once.

After they had finished dessert, Dorcas instructed them all to move into the music room. Caleb carried in the tray of coffee she'd given him. Dorcas pushed him onto a settee upholstered in a pale green brocade and waved Isobel toward one of two grand pianos. "Now you must play for us, dear."

As Isobel settled herself on the piano bench, a white cat half the size of Vincent and Auguste ran out from underneath a cabinet overflowing with music books. The animal leaped onto Caleb's lap.

"Is he named for an artist, too?" he asked Dorcas.

"She," said Dorcas, "is named Clara."

Caleb frowned. He couldn't think of any artist whose first name was Clara.

"Clara Schumann," said Isobel.

Caleb still didn't know if that was someone famous or not.

"Men," said Dorcas in a tone of disgust. "She was Robert Schumann's wife, but even though she was the one who played all his music and made it famous, he gets all the credit."

"He died young, and she edited his works and performed a lot of his piano pieces," said Isobel helpfully.

"He went mad," Dorcas said. "Mad as the March Hare."

"Mad Hatter," said Isobel.

"Whatever," Dorcas said. "I think Lewis Carroll was a bit dippy himself, with all those stories about magic potions and talking chess pieces."

Bewildered, Caleb turned his head back and forth as the conversation went on around him. He wasn't sure how they'd gotten from cats to *Alice in Wonderland* so quickly.

"Anyhow," Dorcas said, "it's plain to see that Clara loves Caleb. That's a very good sign. Very good indeed." She nodded to Isobel. "Play some Chopin for us."

Isobel began to play. The piece sounded familiar to Caleb, but he couldn't identify it. He was certain he'd never heard it played the way Isobel played it, in any case. The notes coming from the piano were achingly beautiful. They surrounded him, filling his head and his heart and, he was sure, working their way into his soul. They made him want to weep and to laugh. He couldn't believe a simple piece of music was evoking this kind of response in him. He had always appreciated music, but had never been a particularly attentive listener or very critical of what he listened to. He had rarely thought of it, when he stopped to think about it at all, as more than a collection of organized sound. Anyone could make music, he had supposed, if they put some effort into it.

But now, listening to Isobel play, Caleb knew that wasn't true. What she was doing not only took years and years of training, it took a special something. A kind of passion. This was emotion; it was…worship. For the first time, he understood what the psalms were saying when they talked about praising the Lord with music. And for the first time, he wished he had the ability to do so.

Suddenly, the music stopped, and Caleb realized he had closed his eyes. He opened them and found himself staring at Isobel. She was looking back at him, smiling, her eyes alight with joy. Here was someone who clearly loved what she did.

When he felt claws digging into his thigh, Caleb tore his eyes from Isobel's and looked down. Clara was kneading his lap with her paws and purring. She rubbed her chin against his hand, then leaped down and dashed across the room to where the second grand piano stood. She bounded from the bench to the keyboard, creating a surprisingly resonant chord, then hopped to the top and slipped inside. There was a muffled twang of the strings; then all was silent.

Caleb stared at the piano, then looked toward Isobel. "Does she do that often?"

Isobel was frowning in the direction of Clara's disappearance. She turned to him. "No, she doesn't because she knows she's not supposed to." She rose and walked over to the other piano. "This is the second-best piano, the one I teach my students on, but still, it's very valuable."

"Cats shouldn't sleep in Steinways," said Dorcas gravely. "Even if they are second best. She only does this when she's very happy, Caleb." She looked at him pointedly, as if it was his fault that the cat was in the piano, then rose and walked over to Isobel. They both peered inside the partially raised cover. "At least she doesn't sit on the strings. I hope she won't have her babies in there."

"She's pregnant?" Somehow, Caleb was beginning to think the idea of cats giving birth inside Steinways was a normal topic of conversation.

"Yes. We're expecting the kittens in a few weeks." Isobel gingerly lifted Clara out of the piano and set her on the floor.

"Speaking of babies," Dorcas said, "let's talk about why you came, Caleb."

Caleb nearly spit out the sip of coffee he'd just taken. He swallowed, then said in a choked voice, "Yes, let's."

"As you know, my dear Edward was an avid collector of old books, particularly those pertaining to the medical field. Some of them are first editions and quite valuable. I will, of course, give you a tour of the library." Dorcas sat on an ornate Victorian chair upholstered in a delicate rose-patterned tapestry. Despite her fragile-looking build, the chair didn't seem to suit her at all. "But first, I'd like to talk about the terms."

"Terms?" Caleb asked cautiously. "Franklin Porter, the library director, told me you were planning to donate the collection. Perhaps there was some miscommunication—"

"No, no. That's true." Dorcas fixed her bright black eyes on him with a steady gaze. "I do intend to donate the books."

"Oh." Caleb wondered why she was studying him as if he

were some previously undiscovered mammal. What was all this leading to?

"However, there is something I'd like in return. I'm not getting any younger, you know."

There was a strangled sound from Isobel, who was back at her seat on the piano bench, but at a glare from Dorcas, the room became silent again. Dorcas turned back to Caleb and looked at him for a long moment.

"I will donate the books to your library, Caleb, on one condition."

"What is that?"

"That you marry Isobel."

TWO

Isobel wanted to scream. She should have expected this. She'd known something was up, what with Dorcas's throwing the two of them at each other and complaining about her advanced age. But even knowing Dorcas as she did, she'd never imagined her grandmother could propose something so outrageous.

She looked at Caleb. His face had turned a rather greenish shade of white, and she thought he might be about to faint. She sprang up from the bench, hurried over to him, and took his hand.

"Put your head between your knees."

He looked at her uncomprehendingly.

"Here." She pressed a hand against his dark brown hair and was about to shove his head down herself when he grabbed her wrist.

He shook his head. "I'm not going to faint."

"Oh. Well, that's good." She wasn't so sure about herself, though. She took a seat in the Victorian chair that matched the one Dorcas was in and gave her grandmother a frown. "Dorcas, what do you mean you want Caleb to marry me? We don't even know him."

"Pish-tosh. When I was a girl, arranged marriages still hadn't gone out of fashion. My own parents would have married me off to someone, but I fell in love with Edward, and they liked him almost as much as I did. Besides, we've already spent two hours with Caleb, and I haven't seen anything I don't like."

Isobel barely restrained a groan. Honestly, Dorcas could be acting perfectly normal sometimes and the next minute come up with the most outlandish notions. She leveled a glance at her grandmother. Dorcas was wearing that stubborn I-know-I'm-right-and-don't-you-dare-contradict-me look. She knew there would be no reasoning with her, at least not tonight, so perhaps the best plan would be simply to ignore her suggestion. Yes, that was it. She would just pretend the topic of marriage had never arisen.

She turned to Caleb and gave him a dazzling smile. "So tell me, Caleb, what kind of hobbies do you enjoy?"

He looked at her as if he thought her as daft as her grandmother. "I, uh, well, I…fish."

"How nice. And what do you fish for?"

"Sharks."

"How lovely to see you two getting better acquainted." Dorcas beamed. "I'll just toddle off to bed now and think about the wedding plans. Don't you worry about a thing," she said with a little wave as she scooped up Vincent and headed for the door. "I'll take care of all the arrangements. Oh, and Caleb, why don't you come back for dinner later in the week, and I'll show you the library."

There was a long moment of tense silence after Dorcas closed the double doors behind her. Then Caleb turned to Isobel. "Just what do you think you're doing?" he asked, glaring at her.

"Me? What are you angry at me for? This was Dorcas's idea."

"You expect me to believe that that sweet little old lady dreamed up a scheme like that on her own?" He rose from his chair and began to pace across the Aubusson rug. "Do you really want a husband that badly?"

"Wh-what!" she sputtered. "I have no idea what you're talking about."

"Right. What is it, you spend all your time in here playing your piano, so you have to have potential suitors brought to the house?"

Isobel felt a hysterical laugh begin to rise and, with an effort, swallowed it back down. "This is crazy. You don't know a thing about me, yet you somehow feel you have the right to cast me in the role of desperate spinster!" Too agitated to remain seated, she paced over to the piano, then turned back to him. "For your information, even if I were looking for a husband, you certainly wouldn't be one of the candidates."

"I'm crushed." He sent her a withering glance, then plopped back onto the settee. Frowning, he stared at the rug. In a calmer voice, he said, "Well, if it is all your grandmother's idea, why? Why does she want you to marry? And what made her choose me for a husband?"

His reasonable tone brought her cautiously back to her seat across from him. She stared into his eyes, which she noticed for the first time were a warm hazel flecked with gold. At dinner she had thought they were a plain brown. Feeling oddly uncomfortable, she redirected her gaze to the aspidistra on the plant stand behind him.

"I really have no idea. Ever since Grandpa died, she's been talking like she's about to follow him, but she's always been very healthy." She frowned. "She's never said anything about my getting married, though. In fact, she always said she thought a woman should be independent."

"Hmm. How strange." He paused. "So what are we going to do about it?"

"Do? Why, nothing, I suppose. It's probably best to ignore the whole thing."

"Ignore it?" He raised his brows. "When she just left talking about wedding plans?"

"Oh, that. Well, I'm sure it will blow over in time. If she brings it up, I'll simply change the subject."

He grinned. "Like you did a few minutes ago?"

She nodded. "Do you really fish for sharks?"

"I've never baited a hook in my life." He glanced at his watch. "Well, I guess I should get going. You're sure we should ignore it?" At her nod, he continued, "Just tell Dorcas I'll give her a call so we can make arrangements for the books."

"All right."

He looked at her, his gaze serious, and took her hand. "Thank you for dinner. And for playing. That was..." He paused and brought his other hand up so that hers was clasped in between. His palms were warm and comforting. "That was beautiful."

Isobel had received many compliments on her talent before, ranging from the enthusiastic cheers of her students to a personal thanks by a senator when she'd soloed with the San Francisco Symphony. But never had anything so touched her as Caleb's simple words. She felt as if he understood the depths of her heart in that moment.

Caleb turned her hand over in his, looking at the palm, running his fingers across the tendons at her wrist. A tingle of something warm and exciting ran up her arm. "A beautiful hand," he said softly. "And so delicate. It's hard to believe these fingers could create something so powerful."

Then he dropped her hand and once again looked at his watch. "Thanks again. Here," he said, reaching into his pocket and pulling out a business card. "Here's my number in case you need to reach me."

Isobel stared at him, eyes narrowed. How could he be stroking her wrist one second, then handing her a business card the next? "Thanks," she said in the coolest tone she could manage. She didn't reach for the card, so he had to set it on an end table. "I'll show you to the door."

She walked quickly from the room, strode across the foyer, and pulled open the front door. "Good night."

He paused on the threshold and smiled. "Good night."

Barely restraining the urge to slam the door shut behind him, Isobel closed it firmly, then crossed her arms and stood there for a moment fuming. Men! She'd never understand them. First he'd had the gall to accuse her of using her grand-mother—her eighty-four-year-old grandmother!—to find a husband for her, then he'd flirted with her, and finally, he'd walked away as if he found her no more interesting than wheat germ or the weather report.

After grinding her teeth a few times, Isobel sighed and relaxed. There was no use in getting all worked up about it. After all, she'd probably never see him again. She smiled. Wouldn't Dorcas get a kick out of the way he'd reacted? She should go up to her grandmother's room, and they could share a cozy chat, the way they often did, and Isobel could tell her all about—

But no, she couldn't do anything of the sort. Isobel sighed again. She had to keep her lips sealed on any subject that came near mentioning Caleb Murphy. Well, that was no great loss. Tucking a stray dark curl behind her ear, she strode back to the music room. It was definitely a night for some Rachmaninoff.

~ ~ ~ ~ ~

Caleb stared at the blinking cursor on his computer screen. The university library database was not cooperating with him this afternoon. He was trying to locate a series of books for a patron about early research on blood diseases, but all the call letters looked like gibberish.

Maybe it was the music. He usually had the portable stereo on his file cabinet tuned to jazz, but today the jazz station was having a Duke Ellington marathon that had begun to grate on his nerves, so he'd switched to the classical station. The only time he'd listened to classical before was when he wanted to get to sleep. So why was he listening to classical now?

He had just gotten up to switch the station when a piano piece started. His hand stilled, and he stood in front of the cabinet, mesmerized. It was the same piece Isobel had played last night.

Isobel. He might as well admit it—she was the reason he couldn't concentrate today. He'd turned on his computer, and the light blue of the screen saver reminded him of Isobel's eyes. When his assistant had come in to bring him a cup of coffee, he'd smelled her pungent perfume and thought of Isobel's light fragrance. When one of the doctors had come in asking him for assistance finding a book for her research on lupus erythematosus, he'd thought that the shade of her hair was nearly the same as Isobel's.

He was pathetic. He'd spent a few hours with her, for crying out loud, and hadn't even talked to her much, since Dorcas had dominated the conversation. And yet he was acting as if he had some crazy fixation with her.

Well, he didn't. He wasn't the type to get fixations. He set his eyes on a goal and very calmly, very logically, plotted the best way to achieve it. He didn't get bowled over by large blue eyes and masses of dark, curly hair and hands that—

A deep voice announced in a monotone that the last selection had been "Nocturne no. 19 in E Minor, op. 72," by Frederic Chopin. Then he gave the name of the performer, who was some foreign guy Caleb had never heard of before. In any case, he was sure the man hadn't played it as well as Isobel had. Caleb looked up toward the ceiling. *Lord, what is it with this woman? Are you trying to tell me something?*

"I don't mean to interrupt."

Caleb jumped and turned around quickly. Franklin Porter, the director of the medical library and Caleb's boss, stood in the doorway.

Caleb cleared his throat. "No, er…that is…please, have a seat."

Porter came in and sat down gingerly in the chair across the desk. A small man with thinning gray hair, prominent cheekbones, and soft brown eyes, he was often mistaken for the meek and mild sort. But Caleb knew better. He also knew that this visit meant something serious was about to happen; Porter didn't believe in socializing, except for the sake of business.

"What can I do for you?" Caleb looked Porter in the eye and tried not to fidget with the stack of papers in front of him.

"You're looking into the Powell collection." It was not a question.

Caleb nodded.

"And?"

Caleb looked away. Did the man know something? "And, uh…what?"

"How is your progress?"

"Well, I completed the acquisition forms. And then I set up a meeting with Dorcas Powell, Dr. Powell's widow." Caleb cleared his throat again. "And then I met with her." A long pause.

"Yes?"

"Mrs. Powell would like to donate the collection to the library."

"Is that a 'but' I hear?"

Caleb met Porter's gaze. "I'm afraid she has some terms attached to her donation."

"What are they?"

"They're, uh…well, she's asked me for a personal favor."

Porter gave him a hard stare but said nothing for a long moment. Then he sighed, sounding almost compassionate. "I hope you're willing to grant her that favor, Caleb. I'll be straight with you. This collection is very important to the library. You see, Dr. Philip Keck, who was a longtime colleague of Dr. Powell, has offered to donate two million dollars to the library for the acquisition and restoration of rare medical books. Which means, of course, that most of the money would go toward the projects you're working on. But he'll only donate it if we acquire Powell's collection."

Porter leaned back in his chair and raised his steepled forefingers to his chin. "That means, Caleb, that we must get that collection. By whatever means necessary."

"Well, yes," said Caleb, starting to feel a bit nervous under Porter's stare. "I hope we can."

"You'd better do more than hope," Porter said flatly. "I was in an administration meeting yesterday. Our budget for next year is being cut by 15 percent. Fifteen percent is quite a bit of money, Caleb. It could mean cutting jobs." He rose from the chair. "I'd suggest you pursue the Powell collection assiduously."

Caleb stared at the open doorway after Porter left. The whole conversation had seemed unreal from the start, but he couldn't have imagined it. No, he hadn't dreamed up the blade-sharp edge in Porter's voice or the knowing stare in those eyes. Almost like Vincent's eyes.

He groaned, thinking about the meeting last night. He'd handled it poorly. He should have gone in, firmly but politely taken care of business, and departed. Instead he'd stayed for an exquisite meal, been charmed by an old lady and her three cats, and listened to music played by the most intriguing, the most—

No, he couldn't think about Isobel now. He had to think about getting the collection or he might as well consider going job hunting, according to Porter. What was the best way to go about convincing Dorcas to donate the collection? Other than marrying her granddaughter, that is.

He sighed and looked at the phone. Who would know the answer to that better than the granddaughter herself? As he dialed the phone, he told himself this was going to be strictly business.

THREE

Isobel shifted the bag on her shoulder and reached for the front door of the San Francisco Centre. The bag swung against her hip, and she heard a tearing noise. Great. This was the third bag she'd ripped in the last six months. Why couldn't anyone make one sturdy enough to carry thirty pounds of music books?

Wrapping her arms around the canvas satchel so nothing would spill out, she hurried toward the curving escalators and climbed on behind a woman wearing a sleek beige suit and a quart of some fruity perfume. Thankfully the woman got off on the third floor, and Isobel moved to the next set of escalators, pinching the bridge of her nose to keep from sneezing.

Nordstrom was located on the fourth through seventh floors, but the piano was on the fifth floor near the Nordstrom Pub. As Isobel climbed onto the next set of moving stairs, she could hear strains from the piano floating down.

Lily Tanaka was at the keyboard this afternoon. The petite Japanese woman often had the shift before Isobel's, and she invariably played American tunes from the thirties and forties. This time it was—Isobel peered at the thick book propped on the piano as the escalator drew closer—*The Best of the MGM Musicals*. If she remembered correctly, the one Lily was playing now was called "For Me and My Gal."

When Isobel stepped off the escalator, Lily nodded and

smiled at her, her shiny black hair swinging. "Hiya, girl. You early today. That not like you."

Isobel checked her watch. It read seven minutes before the hour. That meant she was three minutes late for her meeting with Caleb, since her watch was set five minutes ahead. At least she hoped it was five minutes ahead.

She glanced around. She didn't think he was the type to be late for an appointment. And she was right. There he was in the next department over, women's dresses, waving at her from behind a rack of sequined gowns. She told Lily she'd be back in a few minutes and carefully arranged the tattered bag of music next to the piano.

Lily turned her head without missing a beat in the music and spotted Caleb. "Ah, you meeting a man. That definitely not like you. He pretty cute, though, eh?"

Isobel rolled her eyes. When she'd untangled a long curl from the strap of her bag, she trotted over to where Caleb was sitting at the base of a mannequin that sported a short black silk chemise.

He stood. "Thanks for meeting me. I'm sorry it had to be so sudden. I hope I didn't mess up your schedule or anything."

"Well, I've got a few minutes before my shift. What do you need to talk about? You sounded a little stressed on the phone."

He glanced around, eyeing a couple of women sifting through a nearby rack and loudly discussing their husbands' shortcomings. He looked toward the Pub, which was the only seating area available. Although it was nearly empty this time of day, by the look on his face he didn't think that was a suitable place for them to talk.

"Maybe we could just keep walking around?" he said finally. "It might be a little more private that way."

He made it sound as though they were on a top-secret mission. Wondering what all the secrecy was about, she shrugged and followed him.

They began strolling down the aisle that circled the center of the building, which was open to the curving escalators that stretched all the way to the top floor. Lily was playing some soft, slow piece now, and the sounds of the piano were soothing, almost meditative. The music began to fade as they walked farther away, drowned out by the rustle of bags and chatter of shoppers and salesclerks.

"How is Dorcas?"

Isobel didn't have to ask him what he meant. She knew he didn't mean to be callous, but he certainly wasn't inquiring about her health. "She's not forgetting as quickly as I thought she would. This morning over breakfast, she started talking about dresses and wedding cakes and if I had any idea where you might want to go for the honeymoon."

Isobel felt Caleb's eyes on her, and as she met his gaze, she blushed. Her skin was so fair, she knew she was probably turning pink all the way to her hairline. Good grief, she was acting like a teenager. They were both adults. They should be able to talk about wedding cakes and…and honeymoons. She felt her face grow even hotter.

Where would he go on a honeymoon? Was he the type for active vacations, always seeing things and going places? Or would he want to relax and spend lazy days with her—er, with his wife?

"And what did you tell her?"

Caleb's question startled her from her straying thoughts. "Tell her? What was I supposed to tell her? I don't know what you'd do on your honeymoon."

The moment she said the words, she clamped her lips tight

and knew her face had turned an even brighter red. Even her ears were burning up. When she dared to meet his eyes again, she saw that he was smiling, but not in a lewd way. Rather in a warm, friendly, sharing-a-joke way. Now she could note the exact color of his eyes. They were a lovely brown, the shade of milk chocolate, with generous sprinkles of gold as if the sun had hit just those few spots and left permanent bits of light behind.

"I, uh, well, I just changed the subject the way I was supposed to," Isobel said, desperately hoping her face was returning to its normal color.

"I'm almost afraid to ask what you changed the subject to."

She grinned. "I told her I thought Vincent was having trouble coughing up a hairball and maybe he needed to go to the vet."

"That's a good one. I bet a veterinary emergency would be one of the few things that would distract Dorcas. Did it work?"

"Like a charm. She went off in search of him, yelling that she'd let him sniff oil paints for comfort while the vet checked him out."

Caleb looked startled for a moment, then laughed. "Oh, right. Oil paints, Vincent. And Clara has her Steinway. What does Auguste get, a bronze statue?"

Isobel nodded. "I'm afraid so. A little bronze bust. It's of Aristotle, and certainly nothing comparable to Rodin's works, but Auguste doesn't seem to mind. He actually snuggles up to it sometimes when he naps."

Caleb was glancing at something in the distance and didn't seem to notice that she was watching him. My, but he had a nice profile. Strong brow and chin, straight nose, firm lips.

"So, do you think we're a couple of lunatics?"

He glanced at her, his eyes alight with humor. "Certifiable. But in the sweetest possible way."

"Well," she said dryly, "I certainly can't ask for higher praise than that." She skimmed her hand along the railing, then stopped and looked down at the floors of shops below. "Anyway, it looks like Dorcas may take a little longer than I expected, but I'm sure she'll come around."

Caleb ran a hand through his thick brown hair, then leaned his arms on the railing and stared pensively across the open space. "That's what I wanted to talk to you about." He turned to her, his eyes now dark and serious. "I'm afraid I may not have very much time."

She frowned. "What do you mean?"

"Franklin Porter, the library director, came to talk to me yesterday afternoon. He told me bluntly that the library is having its budget cut, and if I don't bring in this collection, my job could be cut as well."

"What? That—that's blackmail! But why is this particular collection so important? I know Grandpa had some valuable books, but surely they're not vital to the library."

He smiled, a bitter smile. "It's not so much the books as what the books bring with them. A colleague of your grandfather has promised a two-million-dollar gift to the library if we acquire this collection. Money talks, after all. And that much money speaks pretty loudly to the university administration."

"I see." And she did. In the years she'd lived with her grandparents, she'd seen a great deal of what money could do. Not that Grandpa and Dorcas had flaunted their wealth; no, she supposed they would have been the same people if Grandpa had been a plumber instead of a surgeon. But with the reputation Grandpa had acquired in his profession, he had attracted all sorts of people interested in money, from society mavens to fund-raisers. She knew that as a Christian, Grandpa had been concerned about being a good steward of what he'd viewed as

God's money, and she'd seen the headaches it caused him when he struggled over the best use of his talents and resources. Oh yes, she knew well the ways money talked.

It was ridiculous to think that he might lose his job over a bunch of dusty old books. She didn't know why Dorcas was being so stubborn about this. Why was she so insistent that Isobel find a husband all of a sudden? Or perhaps it hadn't been that sudden. Her grandmother had dropped hints over the past several years about seeing Isobel settled and about getting some great-grandchildren to spoil. But she'd certainly never been so overt. Maybe the only way to solve this problem was to play along. As the scheme began forming in her head, she brightened and turned to Caleb with excitement.

"Well," she said firmly, "all this nonsense isn't worth losing your job over. We're just going to have to get Dorcas to sign over the books."

"And how do you propose we do that?"

"By giving her what she wants."

Caleb gaped at her. "Surely you're not suggesting we get married."

"You needn't make it sound so distasteful." She lifted her chin. "Anyway, we don't have to get married; we'll just get engaged. Just for pretend, you understand. I wouldn't want you to have a stroke or anything when you think about marriage to me."

"It's not that—" He stopped and shook his head. "No. It's absolutely out of the question."

"But why? It'll be easy. All we do is tell Dorcas we've fallen in love and want to get married. She'll have a wedding to plan, and you'll have your books. Simple."

"No, it's not simple. I won't deceive your grandmother like that, and I won't use you just to acquire a bunch of books."

"But it's not just a bunch of books; you said your job was on the line. And we don't have to deceive her. We won't tell her we're in love; we'll just say we're engaged. Lots of people get married for reasons other than love anyway."

"Would you?"

"Would I what?"

"Get married for a reason other than love."

Would she? Would she marry someone she wasn't in love with? What was love worth anyway? It only caused pain when the person you loved left or died. Nearly everyone she'd loved was gone. Her parents had loved each other, and so had Grandpa and Dorcas, and now they were all dead, everyone but Dorcas. Her grandmother was all the family she had left, and Isobel couldn't bear the thought of her dying someday as well. She'd do anything if she could prevent that.

She looked up at Caleb. "I love Dorcas," she whispered. "I want her to be happy."

The expression on his face was so tender and gentle at that moment that she felt tears sting the backs of her eyes. He reached out a hand and touched a finger to her cheek and very softly caressed her skin. Isobel wanted to lean into his hand and press her cheek against his palm, to absorb his comfort and strength, but she resisted the urge. She'd never known a man to be so compassionate and strong at the same time. It seemed like an odd combination, and yet it seemed so natural in Caleb.

"I know you do," he said quietly.

Isobel pulled back a few inches and turned her face aside, blinking away the tears. She took a few deep gulps of air, then looked back at him. "So what do you say?"

He gazed at her for a long moment. The air was heavy with the silence between them, and Isobel heard the noise of shoppers as if from a great distance. The gentleness was gone from his eyes now, replaced by a piercing look that made her feel as though all her secrets were laid bare to him.

"And what do we do once I get the books and Dorcas has the wedding all planned?" he asked. "Do we tell her it was all a pretense?"

Isobel looked away. She hadn't thought that far ahead. She really didn't want to lie to her grandmother, but neither did she want to see Caleb lose his job over a few lousy books. This scheme seemed to be getting more complicated by the minute. But it had to be done. She couldn't think of any better plan at the moment, and it wouldn't be that big a deal in the long run. "I suppose we can just tell her we had an argument and broke it off. The argument part certainly won't be a lie."

He stared at her, then smiled. "No, we don't seem to be having any trouble disagreeing, do we? But, Isobel, I don't take marriage lightly. I consider it a precious gift, something sacred that God has given us, and it should be entered into with careful forethought and respect."

She found it hard not to squirm at his words. Deep down, she agreed, but she'd been hoping God wouldn't come into this. It wasn't as though she didn't think God should be part of a marriage, for she did. She'd become a Christian when she was twelve years old one Sunday when she went to church with her grandparents. And all through her teen years, she'd been active and enthusiastic in her service for the Lord. It wasn't until after the death of her parents that she'd felt herself gradually losing touch with God and wondering if he really loved her as much as she'd once thought.

Now this man was purposely putting God in front of her and forcing her to think of the spiritual ramifications of her plan. It wasn't a comforting thought. But she shrugged it off.

"I agree," she said brightly. "And when I do actually get married, I assure you I'll give it a tremendous amount of fore-thought. But we're not going to get married, remember?"

"That's true." He was silent again, and Isobel wondered in passing if they would get this resolved in this decade, never mind that she was probably already making Lily work over-time. "All right, Isobel," Caleb said finally. "I'll do it. But if Dorcas comes out and asks me directly about the engagement, I won't lie to her. And once I get the books and everything's back to normal, I'm going to tell her the truth and pray that she'll be able to forgive us for this."

Isobel let out the breath she hadn't realized she'd been holding. "Okay," she said. "But like I told you, Dorcas is pretty quick to forget about things. I'm sure she'll understand why we did what we did. She might be angry at first, especially if she really goes to all the work of planning a wedding, but she'll for-give us. She wouldn't want you to lose your job, I know."

She straightened and looked at her watch. It read five min-utes after four. She'd be on time after all. Funny, she felt as if she'd been talking to Caleb for much longer than that. "Well, I guess I'd better get to work now." She smiled. "I'm glad we got that all taken care of."

"Wait a minute." Caleb held out a hand. "We just agreed to become engaged. Shouldn't we close the deal with a kiss?"

Isobel's mouth dropped open. She tried to respond, but her vocal cords had apparently been stricken by paralysis.

"Excuse me, are you Isobel Crawford?"

The voice came from Isobel's immediate right, but it didn't register that the woman was speaking to her until she repeated the question. Isobel turned to face a plump gray-haired woman she thought she'd seen in the administration offices of the department store.

"Yes." Remarkably, her voice sounded quite normal.

"A Dr. Schultz just called and left a message for you." The woman's face scrunched up, as if the words tasted sour. "I'm very sorry, dear, but he said your grandmother has just had a heart attack."

FOUR

Caleb followed as Isobel raced up the stairs inside the Powell mansion. He and Isobel had left Nordstrom immediately after Isobel had made sure Lily could substitute for her at the piano. The message from the doctor had said that he'd come to check on Dorcas at home after she'd called him. He was an old family friend, Isobel explained, and he always made house calls for them. That was about all the information Caleb could gather on the hurried drive over here. At traffic lights, he kept glancing at her, worried at the way she cradled a ripped bag to her chest and stared blankly out the windshield. But every attempt at conversation was met by monosyllabic answers. Finally, he gave up and hoped that at least his presence would offer her some comfort.

At the top of the stairs was a landing that matched the foyer downstairs, with the same green marble floor and an Edwardian occasional table topped with fresh flowers. They crossed the landing and started down a hall covered by a plush runner a shade darker than the marble. Isobel stopped in front of the first door on the left, which was open, and the two of them entered a sitting room decorated in yellow and blue rosebuds. Wide double doors led to the bedroom, where they found Dorcas tucked under the covers of an enormous four-poster bed made of gleaming mahogany and topped by a canopy of yellow dotted swiss. Her head was barely visible above the fluffy white comforter, and Vincent, as usual, was nearby, but apparently he had been at least temporarily banned from the bed, for he was perched on the nightstand and looking offended.

After the alarming phone message, Caleb had been preparing himself for the worst, but Dorcas was looking pink cheeked and bright eyed, chatting enthusiastically with an older man who was sitting on a chair by the side of the bed. A black doctor's bag sat on the floor beside his feet.

When Dorcas spotted them, she none too subtly leaned back against the pillows, quit talking, and closed her eyes. Caleb could almost feel the tension drain from Isobel. She crossed over to the bed and stood looking down at her grandmother, her arms folded across her chest.

"Hello, Dr. Schultz," Isobel said. "Hello, Dorcas. Caleb and I were worried when we received the message, but apparently there was no need."

Dorcas opened her eyes slowly. "Oh, hello, my dear," she said in a shaky voice. "I'm so glad you're here. These could be my last moments on this earth."

Isobel didn't answer. She turned to the doctor and asked, "Dr. Schultz, what happened? Did my grandmother really have a heart attack?"

The doctor cleared his throat, obviously uncomfortable. "Well, I—"

"Oh, Isobel," Dorcas interrupted in a much stronger voice. "I'm sure it was a heart attack. I had a pain in my shoulder, just like they say, and I thought I was going to pass out."

Isobel nodded but didn't look at her grandmother. "Well, Doctor? What was your diagnosis?"

Dr. Schultz took off his glasses and began polishing them against the leg of his trousers, studying the process as if it were the most fascinating thing he'd seen in years. "Er, as your grandmother says, Isobel, often a heart attack is manifested by sharp pains in the left shoulder and down the arm."

"That's exactly what it was, Doctor. You've hit it right on the nose," Dorcas said.

"Dorcas, please quit interrupting the doctor," Isobel said politely before turning back to Dr. Schultz. "Please continue."

"Don't you believe Dr. Schultz knows what a heart attack is?" Dorcas demanded. "Surely I've taught you to respect your elders, Isobel."

Isobel frowned at Dorcas. Caleb felt a cat brush against his leg and bent down to pick up Auguste. He watched, fascinated, as the battle of wills continued.

"Grandmother, for someone who has supposedly just had a heart attack, you're acting awfully fit."

"I'm just naturally full of vim and vinegar," Dorcas muttered.

"Vim and vigor," Isobel said absently.

"Whatever."

"So, Doctor, can you confirm that Dorcas did have a heart attack?" Isobel asked.

Apparently Dr. Schultz's glasses were particularly dirty today. He continued to look down as he answered Isobel. "Well, I examined Dorcas and couldn't seem to find anything wrong, but that doesn't mean that she couldn't have experienced a mild angina. We would have to do further tests to make sure."

Dorcas bolted upright in the bed, the comforter falling away. "Oh, I'm sure it's nothing serious. I won't let a mild angina stop me." She began to toss the comforter aside, but Isobel stopped her.

"I don't know, Dorcas, I think perhaps a good battery of tests would be wise. We can't be too careful."

Caleb sat down in a cushy wing chair and stroked Auguste behind the ear. Vincent, having apparently decided that he wasn't getting enough attention, jumped down from the night-stand, hopped to the arm of Caleb's chair, and began batting at the hand that was petting Auguste. Caleb gave one hand to each cat and leaned back. This show was getting more interesting all the time.

Dorcas glared at Vincent's defection, then turned her scowl on her granddaughter. "It's not necessary."

Isobel sat on the edge of the bed and crossed one leg over the other. She was wearing what Caleb guessed was a typical uniform for her Nordstrom stint: slim black trousers, a white blouse buttoned all the way up to its square collar, and a red paisley vest. She swung her leg back and forth, looking at her grandmother as if she had all the time in the world. "And why is that?" Isobel asked.

"I don't think I really had a heart attack," Dorcas said in a much softer voice.

"Oh?" Isobel said. "Did you or did you not have pains in your shoulder?"

"I did."

"So how do you know it wasn't a heart attack?"

"Because it was a pulled muscle instead?" Dorcas sounded like a child who was trying to make up excuses for her misbehavior and not succeeding.

Isobel lifted a brow. "And how would you have pulled a muscle in your shoulder?"

"Because I was moving the refridgerrerph." Dorcas's voice dropped down until it was an unintelligible murmur.

"Did you say refrigerator?" Isobel asked coolly.

Caleb gazed at her with admiration, one hand stilled over Auguste's back. Had she known what was coming the entire time? She was certainly acting as though she had.

"Yes."

Isobel sighed. "Dorcas, why were you trying to move the refrigerator?"

"Because Vincent's toy mouse was caught behind it. And you know how much he likes that mouse," Dorcas said in a pleading tone.

Isobel sighed again. "Honestly, sometimes I wonder who runs this household."

Caleb raised his eyebrows. She had to guess?

"Thank you for coming, Dr. Schultz," Isobel said. "Even if it was a false alarm. Would you care to come downstairs for some refreshments? I think we should let Dorcas rest awhile," she added, staring pointedly at her grandmother.

Dr. Schultz swiped at the lens of his glasses one last time, then stuck them back on his face, adjusting the wire frame over his nose. "Thank you, my dear, I'd love a drink." Without further ado, the doctor stood up, buttoned his jacket, picked up his bag, and left the room.

"You," Isobel said, looking at Dorcas, "stay in bed. I'll check in on you in an hour. No less."

Dorcas grumbled, but Caleb noticed when he turned around to shut the door that she was pulling out a mystery novel from under the covers and patting the bed beside her to encourage Vincent to jump up.

Auguste dashed down the hall, his marmalade coat a blur as he turned the corner and raced down the stairs. Caleb and Isobel followed at a more leisurely pace. "Did you know what she was up to from the start?" Caleb asked.

Isobel shook her head. "She's always been really healthy, but with the way she's been talking about death lately, I've been wondering if she knew something and wasn't telling me. The minute I walked in and saw her, though, I knew she was up to something."

"Moving the refrigerator." Caleb chuckled. "Dorcas is really something else."

Isobel ran one hand along the banister and shot him a sidelong glance. Her eyes were bright, her lips curved just slightly, as if she were trying to hold back laughter. For an instant, Caleb's breath caught in his throat. She was so lovely, and yet her manner was purely unselfconscious. It made her even more lovely.

She did laugh then, pressing one hand against her mouth. After a minute, she controlled her laughter. She turned to him and shook her head again. "Yes, she is, isn't she?" She stopped at the bottom of the stairs. "Would you like a snack or something?" She glanced at her watch. "Oh, it's almost six already. Will you stay for dinner?"

The invitation, both in her words and in her expression, was so appealing that Caleb couldn't even begin to think of any excuse. "I'd love to."

They entered the kitchen, where they found Dr. Schultz staring out the window at the garden, once again polishing his glasses, this time on the sleeve of his jacket.

"Doctor, would you like to stay for dinner? There's some fresh pork tenderloin, and I made a cheesecake this morning."

"Why yes, dinner sounds delightful." Dr. Schultz waved a hand in the direction of the backyard. "If you don't mind, I think I'll take a little stroll in the garden. Your grandmother has such a way with roses, and I see the Old Blush Chinas are beginning to bloom."

"Oh, by all means, go ahead," said Isobel. "And take your time. Dinner won't be ready for at least half an hour."

Isobel put Caleb to work washing and plucking the stems off a bunch of spinach while she began a risotto. Absently, he ran the leaves under the water, watching Isobel as she worked at the stove. Her movements were smooth and practiced as she melted butter in a saucepan, chopped an onion, then tossed the onion into the pan along with some rice. It was funny; he'd seen snippets of cooking shows on TV and always thought them dull, filled with monotonous instructions and dishes that didn't look too appealing. But now, as he watched Isobel stirring the rice and humming under her breath, he was fascinated. She made it look so easy. He had a sudden image of the two of them working together in a kitchen for many meals to come.

Caleb frowned. Where had that thought come from? He had never liked cooking; he'd always thought food a necessary but uninteresting thing, and heating packaged meals in the microwave was quick and painless. He didn't have the slightest idea of how to put a meal together from scratch and didn't particularly care to learn, either. He was only washing this spinach to be polite. Maybe he'd go for a walk in the garden like Dr. Schultz as soon as he finished this.

Isobel glanced over her shoulder at him and smiled. "How's it going?"

Caleb held out the bowl filled with clean, stemmed spinach. "I'm all done. What else can I do to help?"

She gestured him over to the stove. "You can keep stirring this while I work on the meat. Risotto is kind of tedious to make, because you have to stir it the whole time, but it's worth it." She handed him the wooden spoon, then moved to the refrigerator and took out a package wrapped in white paper.

"Isobel," Caleb said slowly, "I've been thinking. Are you sure this mock engagement is a good idea?"

She cast him a sharp glance. "Why do you think Dorcas pretended to be having heart trouble this afternoon?" Her tone was mildly curious, as if she were asking his opinion on the state of the economy.

He shrugged. "To get attention, I assumed."

"Yes, Dorcas likes to draw attention to herself, but she's never used such drastic means before. You don't think it's at all coincidental that she pulled a stunt like that just when she's getting excited about the prospect of my marriage?"

Caleb stared at her, his hands still. Surely Dorcas wouldn't go that far. Would she? "Do you mean she's trying to force this marriage by acting as though she doesn't have much time to live?"

"I'm sure of it."

"But why?"

Isobel rubbed olive oil into the meat. "Dorcas and I only have each other. Everyone else in the family is gone. She was an only child, my mother was an only child, and so am I. I suppose it's natural that she doesn't want me to be left alone. She is eighty-four years old, after all; she won't live forever."

Her tone was light, but Caleb heard a slight catch in her voice. "Isobel—"

"The rice is clumping."

"What?"

"The risotto. You need to keep stirring it."

Caleb looked down at the pan in front of him. There were big lumps dotting the top of the rice mixture. He began stirring vigorously.

Isobel sprinkled salt and pepper over the meat, then turned on the grill set into the stovetop.

"Isobel," Caleb asked cautiously, "what happened to your parents?"

She carefully placed the meat just so on the grill. A long moment passed before she answered. "They died in a car accident. On my twenty-first birthday." She wiped her hands on a towel and looked at him. "I was playing with the San Francisco Symphony. Opening night. Rachmaninoff and Grieg." She smiled faintly. "I felt so grown-up. It was the first time my mother had let me wear anything other than proper black attire. I was in a floor-length satin dress of electric blue, and my hair was up. The symphony was playing their first piece—I don't remember what it was—and I was backstage, feeling nervous and excited, and anxious because my parents hadn't arrived."

She looked away and reached her hands behind her, bracing them against the edge of the counter. "A policeman arrived instead and told me my parents wouldn't be coming. Not ever. It was a foggy night, not that that's so unusual here, but apparently the drunk driver who hit them wasn't used to it." Her voice dropped to a whisper. "He was killed as well as my parents, so I couldn't even blame him. I had no one to blame but myself. If they hadn't been driving to see me perform, if they hadn't stopped along the way to pick up flowers for me, maybe…" She paused. "They'd bought two dozen white roses."

Isobel's voice had become raspy with the strain of holding back tears, and Caleb couldn't stand to watch. He turned off the burner, set the pan aside, and held out his arms. She moved quietly into them.

Her shoulders were tense at first, but they gradually relaxed as Caleb moved his hands in slow, soothing strokes over her back. She buried her face against his neck, but she didn't weep. Her tears were few and slow, but they came, and Caleb knew they helped to ease the pain for her. He ran his hand along the length of her hair and whispered quiet words of comfort.

At last, she drew back and smiled a watery smile. "I didn't mean to spill all that."

He smiled back. "You can spill all you like. I don't mind."

She tore off a piece of paper towel and dabbed at her cheeks. He gently took the towel from her and wiped the edges of her eyes, where her mascara had smeared. He wadded up the paper and tossed it into the trash, carefully weighing his next words. He wanted to know her better, but he wasn't sure how much he should press, particularly when she had revealed so much already.

"I haven't performed since that night." She paused. "Except at Nordstrom, but that's different. That's not music I believe in, if you know what I mean." She glanced out the window at the doctor sniffing roses. "This might sound kind of strange, but when I was growing up, I believed that God had given me the gift of music and that I needed to honor him with it. It was pretty incredible the way he seemed to reward that dedication. I don't mean to sound boastful, but I was very good."

She said it in such a sweet, unselfconscious way, he wanted to grin. Heaven knew, she had enough talent in those beautiful hands that she had the right to boast all she wanted, but from what he'd seen, he'd never known anyone less vain about her abilities than Isobel. "That's not boastful. If God has given you a gift, it would be an insult to him to demean it. And I don't think it's a strange idea at all. I believe God has given each of us gifts."

She shrugged, looking slightly embarrassed. "Anyway, after that night, I felt as though I had somehow done something to dishonor that gift. I was starting to become competitive and proud of my accomplishments, and to be honest, that last year or so, I wasn't playing for God anymore. I was playing to bring myself glory. I guess I thought God took away my parents as punishment, and I couldn't play at all for the longest time. I was angry at God and angry at myself for becoming so arrogant."

She turned away and began to swipe a dishcloth over the countertop. "I know now that God wasn't punishing me and that he didn't take away my parents, but I still have a hard time making myself believe it." She looked up, and he saw that her eyes were growing teary again. "It was even harder after Grandpa died last year."

Caleb nodded. He watched as her fingers clenched around the dishrag. She was visibly exerting control over her emotions, and she was succeeding, but he couldn't resist. He grasped her hands, one of them holding the damp dishcloth, and pulled her into his embrace again. They stood there for a long moment, quietly, and then Caleb began to speak. He wasn't sure if it was what she needed to hear at the moment, but he wanted to show her that he understood, at least a little.

"My parents were divorced when I was less than a year old. My father had custody, and I didn't meet my mother until I was twelve. I didn't even think she was alive. Whenever I asked my dad about her, he'd say 'She's gone' and go back to reading the newspaper or whatever he was doing. I guess I just assumed she was dead."

Isobel's arms circled him tightly, but she didn't say anything.

"One day I heard him mention her name on the phone. I asked him about her again, but this time I didn't let him tune me out. I found out that she was alive and living here in San Francisco and that she had remarried when I was still a toddler. I was so angry at Dad for keeping her away from me that I didn't speak to him for days. Then I insisted on meeting her. I'd had some kind of fantasy that my father had taken me away and that she'd been longing to see me all those years. When I met her, I found out the truth. She hadn't wanted me any more than my father had."

Isobel looked up, her eyes bright with tears. "Oh, Caleb, how terrible."

He touched her cheek softly in amazement. She was actually crying. For him. He felt something twist in his chest.

He smiled, trying to lighten the mood. "Well, to get to the

gist of what I'm trying to say, all of that made me very angry at God. I hadn't particularly been exposed to any kind of religion up to that point, but God was certainly after me in my teen years. It seemed I couldn't get away from him; he just kept turning up everywhere I went, like a dog on the hunt. But I wouldn't have anything to do with him. I figured anyone who set me up with parents who didn't care about me couldn't possibly care about me himself." He shook his head. "But I was wrong. There was an old couple who had been our neighbors all my life, and I spent a lot of time at their house, doing odd jobs for a little spending money. They were the best models of Christ I've ever met. They showed me, through their words and their actions, how much God cared about me—far more than my parents ever could. When I was seventeen, I finally stopped running. I became a Christian the summer before I went to college."

They stood, not saying anything, for what seemed a very long time. Caleb was aware of the birds singing in the backyard garden, the hum of the refrigerator, a damp spot on his shirt where the dishrag had soaked it, the soft sound of Isobel's breathing. He smelled the fragrance of her hair, something vanilla with a little citrus mixed in. She looked up at him, and her blue eyes were wide and dark. Her face lifted, and he knew he couldn't resist the invitation.

"Caleb?" she whispered.

"Isobel…"

"Don't you think you should finish the risotto?"

"The ri—" He smiled and shook his head. "Not just yet."

He lowered his head slowly. She closed her eyes.

"Well, well, well," said Dorcas's voice. "I knew Vincent was smelling more than just pork."

FIVE

everal things happened at once. Caleb and Isobel
jumped away from each other. Caleb rammed the small
of his back into the handle of the saucepan containing
the risotto, and the pan went flying over the countertop,
teetered on the edge, and landed with a splat facedown on the
floor.

Isobel backed up so quickly that she slid the heel of her
foot against the damp dishcloth, which had apparently fallen at
some point—not that she remembered dropping it—and the
cloth glided across the linoleum. Her leg went with it, but the
rest of her did not. She landed with a thud on her rear end.

Vincent, in his frantic effort to reach the risotto, leaped out
of Dorcas's arms and sent her falling back into a chair that was,
fortunately, in a perfect position behind her. She burst out
laughing.

Caleb let out a couple of very unmasculine giggles, then
began to laugh as well.

Isobel glared at them both. She flung out her hand toward
Caleb in a silent demand that he help her up. As he pulled her
to her feet, she said in as even a tone as possible, "Well, I guess
we won't be having risotto tonight."

Caleb and Dorcas laughed all the harder.

Isobel shooed Vincent away from the spill and began to
clean it up. "What are you doing out of bed, Dorcas?" she
yelled, justifying her loud voice to herself by the fact that her

grandmother wouldn't be able to hear her over the laughter if she spoke normally.

Dorcas quit laughing, but she still wore a wide grin. "Why, I told you, Vincent smelled the pork and wouldn't rest until he'd investigated." She winked. "Apparently his timing was a little off."

Isobel was grim as she scooped the gooey rice off the floor. Vincent's timing had been perfect. She had been about to kiss Caleb, for heaven's sake. The man she was supposed to marry! She groaned inwardly. They hadn't even told Dorcas about their engagement yet, and here she was acting as if she really were engaged. Next thing she knew, she'd be falling in love with the man.

With her lips set in a tight line, she rose and walked over to the sink to dump the rice down the garbage disposal, then took out some orzo, a small rice-shaped pasta, as a substitute for the risotto. The trouble was, Caleb's candid sharing of his background and faith were making her rethink the wisdom of this scheme. She hadn't been very dedicated in reading her Bible of late, but she knew it didn't take a Bible scholar to figure out that God said some pretty specific things about the sanctity of marriage.

"Don't let me interrupt anything," Dorcas chirped. "Vincent and I will just go set the table, and you two can get back to whatever you were doing."

Isobel ignored the latter part of her comment and said casually, "Set four places. Dr. Schultz is staying for dinner."

She watched until she was sure Dorcas was out of earshot, then turned to Caleb. "Are you sure about this?" she whispered.

"Sure about—"

"Quiet!" she hissed.

His voice dropped to a whisper. "Sure about what?"

"About telling Dorcas we're engaged. I'm not so sure we should do this."

"Isobel, I thought we'd decided it was necessary for the time being. But if you're having second thoughts, we don't have—"

"Well, I'm just thinking about what you said. How God means marriage to be sacred and all. It's like my music. I don't want to deface God's gift."

"Like spiritual graffiti or something?"

"What?"

"Never mind." He glanced toward the dining room. "So shall we tell her or not?"

She paused. Why couldn't this be black and white? She didn't want to hurt her grandmother, but she didn't want Caleb to lose his job either. And now there was this other factor creeping in, the fact that she genuinely liked Caleb and wanted to get to know him better. After this whole fiasco was over, would things be too awkward for them to have any kind of normal relationship? She nearly laughed at the thought. She had almost forgotten what normal was.

Isobel shook her head. All this indecision was giving her a headache. She didn't feel comfortable about the deception, but she'd go through with it. To save Caleb's job and to give Dorcas a few days of joy, at least. After all, maybe she and Caleb would decide they wanted to make this a real engagement when all was said and done.

Her breath caught in her throat, and she glanced at Caleb as if afraid he could tell what she was thinking. He wasn't even looking at her, though; he was idly stirring the orzo.

"All right," she said at last. "Let's do it. We can announce it at dinner. But once you get the books, we're telling her the truth."

"Agreed."

Caleb stuck out his hand in a formal gesture, and they shook on the deal.

After they dragged in Dr. Schultz from the garden, they sat down to grilled pork tenderloin with green-tomato chutney, orzo, and spinach salad with walnuts. Again, Dorcas was seated at the head, but this time Caleb was next to Isobel, who was at Dorcas's left, while Dr. Schultz sat opposite them. After they had listened to the doctor's rapturous praises of the Old Blush China roses for a good fifteen minutes, Caleb decided that the time was finally right. He wiped his mouth with a linen napkin and cleared his throat.

Everyone kept eating.

Caleb cleared his throat again. "Uh, Isobel and I have something to announce." Isobel dropped her fork as if someone had shot her. Dorcas sat chewing on a breadstick, looking at him with shining eyes. Dr. Schultz looked up, but his eyes had a preoccupied glaze to them, and he continued to spoon bites of orzo into his mouth.

"Yes?" Dorcas prompted.

"Well, after our discussion the other night—" No, that wasn't right. He didn't want to spell it out that he was doing this to get his hands on the books. Surely he could manage a little more subtlety.

"Isobel and I have gotten to know one another, and—" No, that wasn't it either. They'd decided not to pretend they had fallen madly in love. He glanced at Isobel and felt his heart beat a little faster. With all the funny feelings he'd been experiencing the last two days, he *was* beginning to wonder if he was half in love with her already.

He tried once more. "Well, you see—"

"What Caleb is trying to say," Isobel said, giving him an exasperated glance, "is that we've decided to get engaged."

Dorcas dropped her breadstick and clapped her hands together, which startled Auguste, who had been serenely observing the goings-on from a tufted armchair in the corner. He jumped up and ran into the kitchen, no doubt to scavenge for whatever food had been left on the countertops.

"How marvelous!" Dorcas said. She leaned forward over the table, staring at the two of them.

Caleb wasn't sure if it was his imagination or if Isobel had actually leaned slightly toward him, away from Dorcas's intense gaze. In any case, he decided to show his support by grasping her hand under the table. He knew it wasn't his imagination when she held on, squeezing his fingers tightly.

"Isn't that marvelous, Doctor?" Dorcas asked.

Dr. Schultz swallowed and nodded. "Marvelous. If the wedding's soon, you can use some of the Old Blush Chinas for the bouquet."

Dorcas patted his hand. "What an excellent idea. Now, my dears, when shall we have the wedding? They say when you marry in June, you're a bride all your life, but I've always been partial to April weddings myself."

"Well, uh, that is…" Caleb sputtered. "We haven't exactly—"

"Really, Dorcas, don't you think it's a little early to be talking about wedding dates? Caleb only proposed today. We just want to enjoy this time together, don't we, darling?" Isobel shot a dazzling smile at Caleb.

Caleb could have sworn his heart stopped beating for a few seconds. He looked away from Isobel. Maybe he should get Dr. Schultz to take a look at his heart. He glanced back up and realized everyone was silent, staring at him. Isobel was no longer smiling but rather making funny motions with her eye-brows. He understood that he was supposed to say something.

"Yes, that's right," he murmured.

"What nonsense," Dorcas said. "You young people, all you think about is 'quality time' and 'interpersonal relationships.' In my day, that was called marriage. You'll have a lifetime together. Besides," she added, "I want to see a great-grandchild before I die. And that could be any day, as you well know."

Caleb watched with interest as Isobel flushed pink, but she lifted her chin and answered her grandmother in a firm voice. "Dorcas, people don't just have babies on command. Having children is a big decision and one a couple should consider seriously."

"Of course it is. So while you're considering, shall we talk about a wedding date?"

Caleb sighed. It was going to be tougher than he had thought to play out this little charade. And telling Dorcas the truth would take a lot of courage, more than he thought he had at the moment. If only she didn't look so excited at the prospect of a great-grandchild.

"Please, Dorcas," Isobel said. "Won't you give us just a few days to spend time with each other before we get into all the muss and fuss of a wedding?"

Dorcas gave them a long, hard stare, then smiled. "Oh, all right. I'm not so old I can't remember what it was like to be all starry eyed and in love. You enjoy these days of romance, but don't forget, I'll be thinking about the wedding while you're going to drive-in theaters or wherever it is young people go to smooch these days."

Caleb grinned, and Isobel blushed again, a brighter pink this time.

"You've got a deal," Caleb said.

After they'd eaten New York–style cheesecake with raspberry sauce, they once again moved into the music room with a tray of coffee. Caleb poured himself a cup and sat back to enjoy Isobel's music. He had taken only a few sips when he decided he couldn't resist. He got up, went over to the piano, and slid onto the bench next to Isobel. Clara immediately darted out from underneath the music cabinet and jumped into his lap.

Isobel looked at him in surprise but didn't miss a note of the Mozart sonata she was playing.

He leaned over and whispered, "I thought I'd turn pages for you."

She lifted her brows, and he realized she hadn't been looking at the music for quite some time.

He shrugged and grinned. "Well, if you need any pages turned, I'm here." He stroked Clara behind the ears as she leaned into his hand.

"How kind of you."

For the next few minutes, Caleb sat close to Isobel, let the music sink into his soul, and watched as her fingers danced over the keys. They moved smoothly, effortlessly, as if the intricate pattern had been programmed into them. This piece wasn't like the Chopin of the other night with its quiet, haunting theme but instead was light and joyous, with a melody that helped turn his thoughts away from the troubling events of the last two days. Pushing his cares aside, he watched Isobel's hands and simply enjoyed the moment.

Just as Isobel came to the end of a long series of very fast notes, the doorbell rang, and she stopped playing. Dorcas sprang up, disappeared into the foyer, and came back seconds later with a pirate.

Caleb blinked, unsure whether or not he was awake. The

man in the doorway really was dressed as a pirate, complete with knee-length pants torn at the hem, a billowing white shirt, gold hoop earrings, a patch over his eye, and a black tricorn hat.

Dorcas was holding the ruffian by the elbow and grinning. "This is our neighbor, Graham Jennings." She nodded in Caleb's direction. "And Graham, this is Caleb Murphy, Isobel's fiancé. I believe you know Dr. Schultz."

Graham Jennings raised an eyebrow above his patch and looked at Caleb. Then he walked over to the piano, picked up Isobel's hand, and kissed the back of it. Up close, Caleb noticed that the man was in his midthirties or so and might be considered handsome by some women. He frowned. Was Isobel one of those women? He noted that Clara was back under the music cabinet, where she had retreated upon Jennings's entrance. Wise cat.

"Isobel, my dear, your music is absolutely irresistible, as always," Graham Jennings said in a perfectly cultured British accent.

For a moment, Caleb thought the man had some fixation with British royalty as well as an odd manner of dress, but then he realized that the accent was real. He knew some women thought British accents were attractive. Was Isobel one of those women?

Isobel smiled, and Caleb's frown grew deeper. "Thank you, Graham," she said. "What brings you by?"

"Well, I was just heading to a costume party, and as I looked over this way, I saw the lights on in the music room. I just knew you'd be playing something lovely, and I had to see if I could catch a bit of it. I was hoping for Mozart, too, and what luck!—here you are playing Mozart."

"What luck," Caleb muttered.

Isobel stepped on his toes, and when he muffled a yelp, she smiled sweetly at him.

"So this is your fiancé, Isobel?" Graham Jennings lifted the patch and studied Caleb with both eyes. "I must say, the engagement was rather sudden. I don't recall ever seeing you here before—Murtry, was it?"

"Murphy," Caleb said, studying the man in return. "Caleb Murphy." He smiled. "What can I say? Isobel is irresistible."

This time Isobel's elbow connected with Caleb's rib cage. He knew he should be avoiding the topic of engagements at all costs, for they were going to be in enough trouble as it was without spreading the news to the neighbors, but some previously unknown, rather primitive aspect of his nature was egging him on.

"Won't you sit down and have some coffee?" Caleb said. "Dorcas is planning the wedding. Maybe you can help."

"What an excellent idea," Isobel said. Caleb was surprised she could speak at all with her jaw clamped together like that. "And, Caleb, isn't it time you were getting home? I believe you have a book collection you're busy working on, and you don't want to be out too late."

"The books!" Dorcas said. "My goodness, I've been so excited about the wedding, I'd nearly forgotten about the books. Isobel, why don't you show Caleb the library while the doctor and I have a nice chat with Graham. It's been so long since I've talked to a pirate."

Isobel had a mulish expression on her face, but Caleb brightened. This was what he'd been waiting for, the opportunity to study the books. And it didn't hurt that he'd be able to spend some time alone with Isobel. He almost laughed. She'd been trying to get rid of him but instead had inadvertently given him the excuse to stay. And she couldn't argue, for getting him the books was the reason she was going along with this mock engagement in the first place.

"Yes, Isobel," Caleb said softly, taking her by the arm. "Won't you show me the books?"

Isobel nodded but didn't look at him as she led the way out of the room, down the dark hallway, and into the library. As soon as she'd switched on the overhead light, she whirled on him.

"Just what was that all about?"

Caleb looked around the room, searching his brain for a response that would be truthful without inciting any more of her wrath. The library was furnished with heavy, dark, comfortable pieces, and a slightly musty smell hung in the air. This was just what Caleb thought a library should be. Two burgundy leather chairs sat in front of a fireplace with a small chess table between them. A large mahogany desk was in front of the windows, with another leather chair behind it, the kind of chair that was creased and molded to the shape of one person. Caleb could almost see Dr. Powell sitting there, full of vitality, his eyes sparkling with intelligence. The image brought a surprising sting of tears to the backs of Caleb's eyes.

So this was the famous collection, he thought, gazing at the shelves and shelves of books lining the walls. There were the expected leather-bound volumes, many of which were undoubtedly the medical books he had come for, but there were also plenty of paperbacks. Two shelves near one armchair were stuffed with paperback mysteries, their covers tattered: Doyle and Poe, Dashiell Hammett and Wilkie Collins, Christie and Sayers, as well as a number of modern potboilers. Caleb remembered Dorcas's mentioning how her husband liked to sit by the fireplace reading his medical texts. Had he really been reading a text, or had he tucked a mystery inside the covers of another book? Caleb supposed he'd never know.

"Well?" Isobel demanded.

He plucked an early edition of *Gray's Anatomy* off the shelf and began to idly leaf through it as if he were concentrating on nothing more strenuous than digesting his dinner properly. "I was just making conversation," he said, keeping his eyes trained on what looked like an abstract sketch of a fish with its mouth wide open, but was, in fact, a drawing of the muscles of the larynx. *"The muscles which regulate the tension of the vocal cords are the crico-thyroidei,"* he read silently. As he glanced up and met Isobel's accusing stare, he thought he wouldn't mind having something debilitate his crico-thyroidei right this minute.

"You ask a total stranger to plan our wedding, and you call that making conversation?"

He thought of a number of possible excuses, the most reasonable of which was pleading temporary insanity, but then he sighed in resignation. "I'm sorry," he said. "I don't know what came over me." At Isobel's raised eyebrows, he sighed again. "All right, I confess. I guess I got a little jealous, what with his hand kissing and telling you how irresistible you are."

"He said my music was irresistible, not me."

"Your music is a big part of who you are." Caleb put the book back on the shelf, then shoved his hands into his pockets, feeling uncomfortable. "Sometimes when I listen to you play, I think you are your music."

Isobel stared at him for a long moment. Then she suddenly smiled, stretched up on tiptoe, and brushed a kiss over his cheek. "That's the most wonderful thing anyone has ever said to me." She took a step back and folded her arms over her chest. "Why should you be jealous?"

"I just told you. He was kissing your—"

She shook her head. "I know what made you jealous, but why?" She paused. "You remember this is just a pretend engagement, don't you? I hope you're not getting too caught up in your role."

Was that it—that he was getting so immersed in his role as fiancé that he was actually feeling the emotions a normal fiancé would? No, he didn't think that was what was happening. He'd never been that talented an actor. Besides, he'd been having some very confusing feelings about Isobel ever since he'd met her. No, it had to mean—but could it have happened so quickly? He knew it meant he was falling in love, for the first time in his life. *Oh, Lord, what am I getting into? I got engaged to her when I didn't know I was in love, and now that I'm in love, we're going to have to break the engagement. Lord, I need you to give me some wisdom here.*

He realized she was waiting for an answer, but he knew it was too soon to confess his feelings. They'd only met two days ago, and he had no idea how she felt about him. Although there had been that moment in the kitchen…. But they were in the midst of a stress-filled situation right now, with his job at stake and Isobel worrying about her grandmother. They didn't need to complicate all that with romance.

Caleb smiled what he hoped was a smile every bit as charming as Graham Jennings's. "I guess I just got caught up in your music and lost my head for a minute. When you play, I tend to forget about reality." Which was true. He hoped she wouldn't press the issue.

Isobel narrowed her eyes as if deciding whether or not to

believe him. Then she returned his smile. "What a bunch of baloney. But I can never resist flattery about my music." She grabbed his hand. "C'mon, let's look at those books."

SIX

A week later, Caleb was in his office sorting through the notes he'd taken on the Powell collection when his phone rang.

"Caleb, it's Isobel."

He heard the worried tone, and his heart started beating faster. "Isobel, what's wrong?"

"It's Dorcas." There was a catch in her voice. "She's had a heart attack."

After the stunt Dorcas had pulled last week, he had to ask; he wasn't going to rush off to see her because she'd been trying to fetch cat toys from out-of-the-way places again. "No pulled muscles this time?"

"Caleb, I'm at the hospital. They're getting her ready for surgery right now."

Caleb froze. Poor Isobel, she was frantic with worry over her grandmother, and he'd been almost flippant in his response. "I'll be right there."

As Caleb hurried to the hospital adjacent to the medical library, a dozen scenarios played out in his mind, but as concerned as he was for Dorcas, the image that troubled him the most was the thought of Isobel losing yet another person she loved. He didn't know if she could take that right now, and he didn't particularly care to find out. *Please, Lord, keep Dorcas around a little while longer. Isobel needs her.*

And I need Isobel. The thought startled him, even though he knew his feelings for her had been steadily growing. They had spent a great deal of time together in the past week, going through books, talking, sharing meals. He had even gone with Isobel when she took Clara to the vet because the cat had lost her appetite. Isobel had always made it obvious that the cats were only pets, but it was just as obvious that Clara was very special to her. She had held Clara gently while the vet checked her over and pronounced the animal fit but finicky, with her pregnancy progressing normally. While Caleb drove home, Isobel cuddled Clara in her arms and talked softly to make the car ride easier.

Caleb had stayed for dinner several times, sometimes helping with the cooking but more often staying out of Isobel's way and substituting his services as a dishwasher afterward. He didn't particularly care for washing dishes, but he felt he hindered more than helped with food preparation, and besides, he much preferred watching her as she chopped vegetables or sautéed chicken or frosted a cake. His reward always came later in the evening, when they moved into the music room, and Isobel played.

During those evenings, he learned to love the piano, while he had barely acknowledged its existence as a musical instrument before. Sometimes he felt he'd be content to listen to her play forever. He'd always heard about harps and lutes being played in heaven, but somehow he knew that there would be pianos, too. And Isobel would surely be playing one.

He was still troubled about the mock engagement. While he didn't want to deceive Dorcas, he was even more troubled by the fact that, in the midst of such deception, he genuinely cared for Isobel. He knew the situation bothered her as well, but she refused to allow him to say anything until all the details with the book collection were worked out. He'd found himself trying to draw out the process as much as possible as he examined books, made lists, and searched library databases. But unfortunately, he was nearly finished with the preliminaries and would be ready to whisk away the books for end processing with his next visit. And then the truth would have to come out.

Revealing the truth meant the end of his time with Isobel. And although they had known each other for just over a week, he didn't know if he could handle never seeing her again. Now, with Dorcas seriously ill and going into surgery, things had changed. Even if Dorcas had a swift recovery—and he prayed that she would—he couldn't exactly continue on with what he was doing as if everything were hunky-dory. But could they tell Dorcas the truth now? He didn't want to risk endangering her health even further by giving her that kind of shock.

He hurried up the walk to the hospital's main entrance, dreading what he'd find inside.

Thankfully, the surgery was successful, and Dorcas was recovering in timely fashion. After three days, however, Isobel fervently hoped she'd never see a hospital again once Dorcas was well. She rubbed a hand wearily over her eyes and let the book fall shut in her lap, then looked at her watch. Dorcas had been napping for only twenty minutes now, but it seemed like forever. Of course, she had been doing quite a bit of sleeping lately, so it hadn't been all that long since the previous nap. Isobel wanted to stay until visiting hours were over, but the three days since her grandmother's surgery had been long and stress-filled, and she desperately needed a nap herself.

On top of her normal schedule of piano lessons and playing at Nordstrom, she had been spending many hours a day at the hospital and, in the last day and a half, had been scurrying around trying to fulfill the to-do list Dorcas had given her. Isobel leaned her head against the wall and closed her eyes. She had never realized how much Dorcas did to keep up the house. Despite the cleaning service and gardener, who each came once a week, there were a hundred little things that needed to be done, and Isobel had always taken for granted that they would be taken care of. But now that Dorcas wasn't around to keep everything in order, suddenly all the cats needed continual feeding, all the bills were coming due at the same time, the plants were wilting, and on top of everything, she'd had to ask the paper boy to come back to collect his payment because she'd lost her checkbook and had only three dollars and twenty-six cents in cash.

She opened her eyes and leaned forward, resting her arms against the stiff fabric of the hospital sheets. She gently wrapped her fingers around Dorcas's thin, blue-veined hand. Despite its frail appearance, the fingers were still strong, even in sleep. It was comforting to know that her grandmother still had some time left on earth. Isobel didn't suppose she'd ever be ready to say good-bye to Dorcas, but this past week or two had been particularly special. Ever since Caleb had entered their lives, the days had taken on a brighter hue, almost as if every lightbulb in the house had been taken out and replaced with one of a higher wattage.

She smiled, thinking of how much she'd come to depend on Caleb during the past three days. He had been rock steady, always there when she needed him and always knowing what she needed to hear. To think he had only come to collect some books. Little had he known what he was signing on for when he'd agreed to this engagement charade. And he hadn't even gotten the books yet.

A light tapping sounded at the door. Isobel turned her head and saw Caleb. He was wearing his work clothes, a pair of khakis and a blue oxford shirt, cuffs unbuttoned and rolled up, and he was carrying his briefcase. She glanced at her watch again. It was only four o'clock. Had he left work early just to come see Dorcas? The sweetness of it made her smile.

He came to stand next to her. "How's she doing?" he whispered.

Isobel put a finger to her lips and gestured for them to step outside. Once they were in the hallway, she pulled the door toward them so that it was only slightly ajar.

"She's doing really well," she said quietly. "Of course, she's still sleeping a lot of the time, but the doctors say everything looks good, and she should be able to go home in another three or four days if she keeps improving so quickly."

"That's great." He rubbed a thumb gently over the shadows below her eyes. "But you don't look like you've been taking care of yourself too well. How much sleep have you had in the last three days?"

She shrugged. She should have known he'd notice and comment. "I'll be all right. I've just been busier than usual lately. But I won't fall apart; I'm not exactly delicate, you know."

"I know you're not. But right now you look like a soft breeze could knock you over."

"Don't be silly. I—" She stopped as she heard a noise inside the room. She pushed the door open and hurried to the bed.

Dorcas was awake and fumbling with the water pitcher on the bedside table. She looked up and smiled when she saw Isobel and Caleb. It wasn't quite her old mischievous grin but it was enough like it that Isobel felt a sudden rush of relief. And exhaustion. It was as though her body had been waiting for some solid evidence that Dorcas was going to pull through,

155

and now that that smile had provided it, all the hours of lost sleep rushed in and made themselves known.

"Hello, my dears," Dorcas said. "Have you been spending some quality time together?"

Yes, Dorcas was definitely well on her way to recovery. Isobel grabbed the water pitcher and cup, grateful for something to keep her busy.

"Hello, Dorcas," Caleb said. "You're looking much more chipper than when I saw you yesterday. Isobel says you're going to be going home in a few days."

"Yes. Caleb, have you gotten all the books yet?"

Caleb looked flustered. "Well, no, I...that is, I was almost ready to box them up when..."

When Dorcas had the heart attack. He didn't need to finish the sentence, for they all knew what he'd been about to say. Isobel looked at him closely. Was his expression embarrassment over the awkward situation, or was he impatient because he'd lost so much time in getting the books? She couldn't tell. After all the time they'd spent together, she didn't think he'd be so shallow as to be concerned about the books at a time like this, but he did have his job to consider, after all.

Caleb looked at her then and smiled, a sweet, tender smile, and she felt that he somehow knew what she'd been thinking. She was caught in his gaze, unable to tear her eyes away, and she could only stare into his eyes, which were filled with understanding and compassion. He knew her suspicious thoughts, but he didn't condemn her for them. He understood. And she knew that he cared, cared more about her and Dorcas than he ever had for the books or for the job that was depending on those books.

Dorcas cleared her throat lightly, a subtle gesture for her, Isobel thought.

"Isobel, why don't you sit down?" Dorcas said. "You look tired, and I have something I want to tell both of you."

Isobel sat down warily. She had no idea what was on Dorcas's mind, but she had the feeling it was going to be something she'd want to be sitting for.

"I've spent a lot of time thinking in the past three days," Dorcas began. She looked from Isobel to Caleb. "And when you spend so much time thinking at my age, you start to see pretty quickly what your mistakes are. I've made a lot of mistakes in my life, some that I've learned from immediately and some that have taken a little longer. Like the time your grandpa said I wasn't mechanically inclined and I decided to prove him wrong by taking apart the dishwasher and putting it together again."

Dorcas stopped, frowned, then looked a little sheepishly at the two of them. "Though I don't suppose you want to hear that story right now."

Isobel shook her head, wondering if Dorcas *had* a story she wanted to hear right now.

"Well, I guess I'd better get to my point, then." Dorcas glanced down at her hands, which were pleating the sheet into a makeshift accordion. She seemed nervous, a state Isobel couldn't recall ever having seen her grandmother in before.

"Dorcas, what is it?" Caleb asked gently.

She looked up at him. "Please don't be angry. That is, I know you have a right to be angry, but I hope you'll understand what I was feeling and not—"

"Dorcas," Isobel interrupted, "it's all right. Just tell us. We won't get angry." She said a quick prayer for forgiveness after that little lie. Dorcas might make her angry, but she wouldn't express it, not while her grandmother's health was so fragile.

"All right, then." Dorcas turned to Caleb. "When I asked

you to marry Isobel, I shouldn't have. You see, I know I'm an old woman and don't have a long time to live, and I so want to see Isobel settled and starting a family of her own before I pass on. She's been alone for so long, even before her parents died, really, because she's always been such an independent girl."

"Dorcas," Isobel said, "I don't think—"

"No, let me finish," said Dorcas. "This is something that needs telling."

Isobel nodded. She didn't want to interrupt if Dorcas felt she had to tell this. She could only listen and hope that her grandmother wouldn't reveal anything too embarrassing.

"Before Edward died, he and I talked about this together. You see, dear," Dorcas said in an aside to Isobel, "I wasn't the only one who liked to meddle. One day Edward mentioned a young man he'd met, a young man who seemed to be honest, intelligent, and kind, and who possessed a goodly amount of common sense. You may not know this, but common sense is one of the few things we could use a little more of in our family." She nodded, as if she had just made an enormously profound statement.

Caleb raised his brows. His expression was serious, but Isobel could see a twinkle of amusement in his eyes.

"And most important," Dorcas said, "the young man was a Christian. 'Dorcas,' Edward said to me, 'I think this Caleb Murphy is just the sort of fellow our Isobel needs.'"

Both Isobel and Caleb stared at her. Caleb? Grandpa had wanted to set her up with Caleb? Isobel closed her mouth when she saw how wide Caleb's was gaping. She'd had no idea Grandpa had been trying to matchmake or that he'd picked Caleb out for her all those months ago. She hadn't even known Caleb knew her grandpa personally.

"Of course, after Edward died so suddenly, I sort of forgot

about finding a husband for Isobel. My dear Edward," Dorcas said, dabbing at her eyes with a tissue. "He was everything to me. And I wanted a man for Isobel whom she could love every bit as much." She looked up at Caleb again. "As you know, Edward had wanted his medical books donated to the library, and so I called about it and was told someone would take care of everything. Well, when you called me to discuss the books, I recognized the name immediately. And I just knew God had a hand in it."

She shook her head. "I'm afraid that's when I got a bit impatient. All that Edward and I had talked about came back to me, and I was excited to carry it through. So I decided to take things into my own hands, and I blurted out a proposal before the two of you had even gotten to know each other. That was wrong."

Dorcas held out a hand to each of them. The room was still, almost heavy, with the air smelling of that combination of antiseptic and artificial scents unique to hospitals. Isobel heard the hum of the monitors next to the bedside, the monitors that were keeping careful watch over Dorcas. How she loved her grandmother. She didn't always agree with her, but she loved the way Dorcas was always concerned for those she loved, the way she actively pursued whatever she thought would make others happy.

Isobel leaned forward and clasped her grandmother's hand, holding on tightly. Yes, she was angry, but it was more out of frustration than resentment. Dorcas had tried to do what she thought was best and had taken things a little too far. Isobel hoped her touch showed now only that she supported and loved her grandmother very much. The rest could wait until later, when Dorcas had her strength back.

Caleb came and took Dorcas's other hand. He was smiling,

but Isobel couldn't read his expression.

"I want to say I'm sorry," Dorcas said, "and ask your forgiveness. I shouldn't have interfered with your lives like that. Oh, and Caleb," she added, "you can have those books anytime you want. No strings attached."

Isobel felt the sting of tears. Her grandmother was a stubborn woman, and she knew it hadn't been easy for her to ask for their forgiveness. She leaned over and wrapped her arms carefully around the thin shoulders. "I forgive you," she whispered. She felt Dorcas's arms squeeze tightly. When she straightened, she saw that her grandmother's eyes were wet.

Caleb had stepped back from the bed and was looking as though he'd gotten trapped in the lingerie section of a department store and couldn't find the exit. When Dorcas looked at him expectantly, he said softly, "Of course I forgive you, Dorcas." Looking slightly more at ease, he patted her hand. "I understand that you did it because you love Isobel. You didn't intend to hurt either of us."

Dorcas patted Isobel's cheek and beamed at Caleb. "But now that the two of you have fallen in love and decided to get married on your own, everything's worked out just fine."

Caleb cleared his throat and shot a worried glance at Isobel. She shook her head slightly. It was too early for them to tell Dorcas the truth; they'd have to wait until she was a little stronger.

He nodded and looked back at Dorcas. "Yes, of course. Funny how things seem to fall into place." He paused. "I, uh...I think I'll leave you two alone now. I'm sure you have lots to talk about."

"Well, you don't need to rush off," Dorcas said. "You're welcome to stay a while. We can all chat and get to know each other better." She winked.

Isobel suppressed a groan.

Caleb smiled and picked up his briefcase. "Thanks, but I think it would be best if I left now. I'll come visit later, okay?"

And with that, he was gone. Isobel couldn't help but wonder if she'd ever see him again.

SEVEN

Caleb knocked lightly on the open door to Dorcas's hospital room. She had changed rooms since he'd been here last, on the day Dorcas had confessed. This room wasn't as bright and new looking, and the view from the window looked out on another wing of the hospital. Perhaps they saved the nicer rooms for those who needed all the help they could get in their recovery.

Dorcas looked up. "Caleb! I'm so glad you came. I'm getting out of this asylum today, and I'm desperate for company." She set aside a crossword puzzle and folded her arms expectantly, as if she were waiting for him to pull out a bag of magic tricks. Today she was wearing a bright purple sweat suit, which was a refreshing change from the hospital gown.

"Desperate?" He smiled and took a seat next to the bed. "So if a coat rack had walked in here and started talking, you'd have been satisfied?"

She waved a hand absently. "Why haven't you come to visit me sooner? Isobel has been here all the time." Her eyes narrowed. "That isn't why, is it? Are you avoiding her?"

Caleb shifted uncomfortably.

"Don't think I don't know something's going on between you two. I'm not completely batty." She lifted a brow.

Caleb brushed a piece of lint off his trousers. He wished he'd thought to smuggle a cat or two in here, just to give her some distraction. "So, Dorcas, what time are you being discharged?"

"Four o'clock, and don't change the subject. I'm right, aren't I?"

"Right about what?" Despite his casual tone, Caleb could feel his cheeks growing warm.

"Aha!" Dorcas snapped her fingers as though she'd just uncovered the final clue to a mystery. "I knew it, you are interested in each other."

This time, Caleb was the one whose eyes narrowed. "Do you mean you were trying to bluff me?"

She nodded smugly. "It worked, didn't it? You may try to hide behind your words, but the expression gives you away every time. You've got a very honest face, my boy."

"You say that like it's something to be ashamed of."

"No, no, that's good, but sure makes it hard to play poker."

Caleb shook his head, beginning to experience the confusion he'd learned was part of all his conversations with Dorcas. "I'll try to remember that."

"So what are you going to do about it?" Dorcas leaned forward, her eyes intent.

"Do about what?"

"About Isobel, of course. Don't be dense. I know you're in love with her."

Caleb leaned back in his chair and stretched his legs out before him. He'd tried the distraction tactic that Isobel had said usually worked. Now what? Maybe he could use the laid-back approach. "And how do you know that?" he asked. Unfortunately, he didn't quite achieve the blasé tone he was striving for.

"It's as obvious as this crossword." She picked up the puzzle book and waved it for effect. "By the way, do you know a six-letter word that means incorrigible? Starts with *u.*"

Dorcas, he thought, but aloud he said, "How about *unruly?*"

"Thanks." She jotted down the word, then set the book down again. "It just so happens that dear Graham—you remember my pirate neighbor, don't you?"

Caleb nodded. In his opinion, this pirate guy seemed to be turning up all too often.

"Well, dear Graham came by, and we had a nice chat. He's an investment banker and was telling me all kinds of amusing things about Wall Street. He has such a sense of humor."

Investment banker. It figured.

"Anyway, Graham told me that every time he heard Isobel playing, it was Rachmaninoff. She always plays Rachmaninoff when she needs to work off some steam. Poor Graham. You know how he loves Mozart."

Poor Graham indeed.

"And not only that, but every time I mention your name, she snaps at me. Now I find out that you've been staying away from the hospital because she's here." She shook her head. "I know just how it is. Dear Edward and I went through that melancholy period in our courtship. Turns out we had each misunderstood some silly thing and were too proud to be the first to approach the other. Now, why don't you tell me all about it?"

How could he begin to explain the mess he and Isobel had created? They had vowed to confess the truth of their engagement to Dorcas when the time came. Well, that time had come, and he had no idea what to say. It was much more difficult than he'd expected, this business of admitting he'd made a muddle of things.

"Dorcas," he began hesitantly, "you're not the only one who made a mistake here. You see, when you told me I had to marry Isobel to get the book collection, I'm afraid I didn't take the news very well."

She nodded encouragingly. "I don't doubt it."

"And, well, at first Isobel and I were going to try to get you to donate the books anyway. We hoped you'd forget about the whole thing if we avoided the topic." He rubbed his palms over the crease in his trousers, embarrassed at how terribly he'd underestimated Dorcas.

"Not a wise move," Dorcas said gravely.

"No, it wasn't. We soon discovered that that wasn't going to work, and…well, the truth is, we decided to fake an engagement so that I could get the books." He dropped his gaze, unable to maintain eye contact with her.

"You wouldn't have done it if your job hadn't been in jeopardy, I'm sure," Dorcas said.

He jerked his head up. "What?"

"I know you have too much integrity to pull a scheme like that unless you had a very good reason."

"Well, I hope so, and Isobel agreed because she truly wanted to make you happy. But how did you find out?"

"Isobel told me."

"She did? But we were going to tell you together, right after—" His voice dropped to a near whisper. "Right after you agreed to give me the books."

"Ah, there it is. Right after. What is today, Friday? I believe it was Tuesday when I told you to take the books." Dorcas made an exaggerated show of counting on her fingers. "That makes three days in which you could have come to me with Isobel and confessed. But no, you stayed away, and Isobel finally worked up the courage to tell me last night. By herself, mind you."

"I'm sorry," Caleb said, feeling as puny as he had in the third grade, when he'd splashed paint all over the class art project and let his best friend take the blame. Even though the project had looked like something out of a Salvador Dali night-mare and the yellow paint was an improvement, he hadn't been left with a very satisfactory feeling in the end.

"I accept your apology," Dorcas said, nodding primly. "The question is, will Isobel?"

Would she? Caleb wouldn't blame her if she decided to hold a grudge for a while. He couldn't believe how thoughtless he'd been. After Dorcas had offered him the books, he hadn't wanted to come right away and collect them, making it look as if that were the only reason he'd become friends with the two of them. Frankly, he didn't particularly care if he got the books or not, not anymore. Even if it meant sacrificing his job. He'd also wanted to stay away as a show of respect to both Dorcas and Isobel, to allow them to spend time together while Dorcas healed from her surgery. He'd never meant to hurt Isobel. He could only pray that she would allow him to explain and that she would forgive him for getting her into this mess in the first place and then leaving her alone to talk her way out of it.

"So, what are you going to do to show her you're sorry?" Dorcas was chewing on the end of her pen and watching him closely.

"What do you mean?" Caleb stared at her blankly. "I—I guess I'll just explain my reasons for not being here and apologize. Isn't that enough?"

Dorcas laughed. "Oh, my dear, you've got a lot to learn. If I know Isobel, and I do, she has no idea that you love her. She's probably thinking that you got what you wanted, and now you've deserted her. Don't forget that she's lost a lot of people in her life, and she's pretty quick to pull inside her protective shell if she thinks someone might hurt her."

Caleb felt even worse. How could he have known a simple error in reasoning would cause so much trauma for Isobel? He had truly wanted to be considerate of her, and look where that had gotten him. It was enough to make a man quit trying to be sensitive.

He looked at Dorcas. "Do you have any suggestions?" he asked hopefully.

"You have to do something dramatic. Be willing to make a fool of yourself."

He raised a brow. "Is that it? I've been acting like a fool half the time, ever since I met Isobel."

Dorcas shook her head. "No, not idiocy. I mean play the fool, show her you love her and you don't care if the whole world knows it. There's something so endearing about a man who does something to embarrass himself in the name of love."

"Oh." Caleb could feel his throat tighten. He tugged at his collar and stared at the floor for a long moment. He'd never particularly liked public performances, even if he was behaving in a perfectly respectable manner. He'd often wondered if it went back to the time in the sixth grade when he'd played Mercutio in a school performance of *Romeo and Juliet*. During the sword fight, he'd gotten his blade stuck in the cuff of his pants and tripped, doing a clumsy somersault and landing flat on his back. The other kids had made jokes for weeks afterward about "Murphy the Circus Clown."

To embarrass himself publicly, and to do it on purpose, was a nauseating prospect. "Surely she'll understand if I take her out to dinner, maybe buy her some flowers?"

Dorcas looked at him, shrugged, then picked up her crossword-puzzle book. "I suppose she will." Silence filled the room for what seemed like forever. Then Dorcas looked up. "But nothing will convince her as well as making a public declaration."

Could he do it? Well, he supposed the experience wouldn't

be fatal. *Would* he do it? There was no question he had to talk to Isobel and convince her to forgive him, for to lose her forever was a terrifying prospect. Well, why not? He'd been playing it safe all his life. And he'd done more bizarre things in the past two weeks than he'd done in the rest of his lifetime, so he might as well add one more to the list.

He sighed, feeling as if he were playing a role in a sitcom written by Dorcas. "I take it you have something in mind?"

Dorcas sent the puzzle book flying. "Just so happens I do. Now, Isobel will be doing her shift at Nordstrom tomorrow...."

Isobel ran her fingers over the keys, letting the last few notes of the Liszt etude resonate. It wasn't the type of piece she normally played at Nordstrom, since the patrons preferred music more along the lines of Andrew Lloyd Webber's greatest hits, but today she needed the comfort of the familiar.

She had needed that quite a bit in the past couple of days. Ever since Caleb had failed to call or stop by or even leave a message for her at the hospital and she had realized she'd probably never again hear his warm laugh or watch the way he closed his eyes, seeming to absorb her music. Never again. He'd gotten permission to take that cursed book collection, which meant his job was secure, which meant he didn't need their mock engagement as a bargaining chip. He hadn't even had the decency to stop by to say thanks. In fact, he hadn't stopped by at all, even for the books, but she supposed he'd send some lackey to come pick them up. No need for his august presence.

No matter that he had promised to tell Dorcas the truth once he'd gotten his hands on the books. After Isobel had realized that he wasn't going to fulfill that promise, she'd spilled out the whole story to Dorcas. Her grandmother had had the nerve to be understanding and to tell her Caleb probably had a good reason for not coming by to see her. *Humph.* Probably because he'd gotten a big fat bonus for acquiring this collection, and trying to decide how to spend it was taking all his spare time.

Isobel closed the book of etudes and leaned over to stuff it into her music bag. When she straightened, Lily was standing in front of her.

"Lily, what are you doing here? You already did your shift today."

Lily grinned her winsome smile and waved Isobel off the bench, then sat down. "I know. This is special music." She tugged the bench an inch or two closer to the piano and leaned over to check the position of her feet at the pedals. "No, no, don't look." She pressed some sheet music against her chest and shook her head. "This is surprise."

"Surprise? What are you talking about?"

"You find out in a minute."

If Lily smiled any wider, her cheeks might crack, Isobel thought. But she didn't have much time to think, for just then an enormous bouquet of red roses was thrust in front of her face, and a familiar voice said, "These are for you."

Isobel took a deep breath of their sweet scent and considered whether she should thank him before she chewed him out for breaking his promise. The flowers smelled exquisite, and she was afraid that, despite her resolve, she might give him only a lecture, not a chewing out.

"Now stand right there," Caleb said when she turned around to look him in the eye while she delivered her lecture.

Before she could utter a single word in response, he had grabbed her by the arm and was positioning her just so a few steps away from the piano. Then he stood next to Lily and whispered a few words into her ear.

Isobel frowned. Just what was going on here? A few people were giving them curious looks as they walked past. This wasn't a very good setup for a lecture. Maybe she'd just have to berate him in a low voice.

Caleb straightened and clasped his hands in front of him as if he were an operatic soprano about to begin an aria. Lily began playing some tune with a syncopated beat that sounded vaguely familiar. Caleb squinted at the music and seemed to be counting out beats. Isobel felt her heart give a spastic thud. He looked as if he was going to sing.

She held out a hand to stop him, but it was too late. Caleb tapped his toe a couple of times, took a deep breath, and looked at her. *"You made me love you. I didn't want to do it; I didn't want to do it."*

He was singing. Not just singing, but singing a love song. For her. Isobel blinked her eyes and cradled the roses closer. This was actually some sort of apology, and—he loved her.

"You made me happy; sometimes you made me glad. But there were times, baby, you made me feel so bad."

Isobel smiled, her breath catching on a funny lump in her throat. He didn't have too terrible a voice, but it wasn't a simple song. There were lots of difficult intervals. But she didn't care if he couldn't sing; she didn't care if there was a crowd forming around them; she didn't even care that water from the roses was dripping down the leg of her pants.

"Give me, give me what I cry for; you know you've got the kind of kisses that I'd die for. You know you made me love you."

Caleb ended the verse, his voice wavering in a slight vibrato, on a note that was obviously too high for his range. Lily leaned over the keyboard and exuberantly launched into the bridge for the next verse. But Caleb stepped forward. The crowd seemed to lean in as if they were anticipating the climax to some melodrama.

He took the flowers from her and set them on the piano, then held her hands between his. "Isobel, I'm sorry I wasn't there for you when you told Dorcas the truth."

Isobel looked into his face intently. There was a slight flush along his cheekbones, the only evidence that he was aware of their audience. His eyes were dark and serious and filled with such sincere emotion she felt the lump grow even bigger in her throat. She nodded slightly, encouraging him to continue.

"I'm sorry, too, about this whole elaborate scheme we cooked up." He shook his head, his hands tightening around hers. "Oh, not because of the time I spent with you. In fact, I'm amazed and so thankful to God that he worked everything out to bring us together. The books, my job, even Dorcas's proposal. It was all a miracle.

"But I'm sorry if I've ever led you to believe I was only in this for the books. In fact, I don't care if the books ever make it to the library, even if it means losing my job." His voice dropped to a low, soft pitch, almost like a caress. "What I care about is you. Isobel, I know we've been through all kinds of strange things in the past couple of weeks. It's certainly not been the conventional kind of courtship, what with our getting engaged before I even asked you to marry me."

Isobel stared up at him through the sheen of tears in her eyes. She could hardly believe she was hearing these words from his mouth, just minutes after she'd been so angry with him she'd been planning her lecture. She couldn't recall a word of that lecture now.

Caleb raised one hand to touch her cheek, then reached back to smooth a curl behind her ear. "Isobel, I love you. And I know we don't know each other very well, but will you agree to let us get to know each other better, with the hopes that someday we can turn our fake engagement into a real one?"

She laughed. "Is that a proposal?"

"It most certainly is."

Isobel had always thought it a cliché, but now she knew exactly what it meant to have joy bubble up inside. She wrapped her arms around him and tilted her head to look into his eyes. "Then I accept."

He sealed their agreement with a kiss as the crowd showed their approval and Lily warbled the rest of the song.

"I want some love, that's true. Yes, I do, 'deed I do, you know I do."

She did want love, Isobel thought as she drew back and smiled at Caleb. And she had it.

EPILOGUE

Caleb poured a cup of coffee from the silver pot and handed it to Dorcas, then poured one for himself. He leaned back on the little green settee and patted his lap. Clara jumped up.

He smiled at Isobel, who was engrossed in a Beethoven sonata. She hadn't played any Rachmaninoff since they'd gotten engaged. Engaged for real, that is. That had been nearly two months ago.

Their wedding was set for next week, and Dorcas had been running around making plans for it in a state of constant euphoria. She had made a remarkable recovery from her surgery and said she felt better than new. The doctors agreed that all this wedding business seemed to have been good for her heart. The only ones to suffer had been the cats, who weren't getting nearly as much attention as they were accustomed to, and both Vincent and Auguste made it clear that they didn't like their deprivation. Amazingly, Dorcas didn't seem to pay any mind to their complaints, and once Caleb had even come across her scolding Vincent. Clara kept to herself as usual, except when Caleb was around, and then she became the most affectionate of animals.

Caleb had delivered the books as promised to the medical library, then, with the full support of Isobel and Dorcas, had taken a job with the city library. It was an enormous change from the intensity of academia, but he loved it. He sometimes wished he'd made the move earlier, but then he reminded himself that God had brought everything about in the right time. Isobel was the perfect reminder of that.

How he loved her. And he came to love her more every day, just when he thought he couldn't possibly love her any more. She was playing more than ever now. Although she had quit her work at Nordstrom, she continued to give music lessons and was practicing for her own professional engagements. She would be doing some soloing starting in the fall with a few orchestras around the Bay Area. She even talked about playing with the San Francisco Symphony again someday. "If they'll take me," she'd added with a laugh. But not long after she'd said that, the manager had called and asked if she'd be interested in doing something for them next season. He'd heard she would be performing with the Palo Alto Chamber Orchestra and was thrilled that she was "back on the circuit."

Caleb and Isobel agreed that they would discuss it before she even considered any offers outside the local area, but Caleb loved to see her performing and didn't mind if it took her to China if he could see her doing what she loved. He knew the day might come when that possibility could be very real, though, and he wasn't sure he'd be able to bear having her so far away too often. But for now, he didn't think he could be any more content. His life was truly blessed.

He took a sip of his coffee and petted Clara. She arched under his hand, purring loudly, almost in rhythm with the music. She'd had her litter, four adorable kittens that were a mixture of white, black, and orange, so it was difficult to tell who the father was. The kittens were now eight weeks old. The three of them had discussed finding homes for them, but none of them liked the idea of giving away the creatures that had already become a part of the family.

Isobel came to the end of the piece and looked up. "Any requests?"

"Won't you play the Brahms, that really loud one?" Dorcas asked. "Johannes was such a passionate man. They say he was in love with Clara, you know," she said in an aside to Caleb.

"No, I didn't know." Caleb had ceased to be startled when she talked about long-dead composers and artists as if she'd known them.

"I'll see if I can find it," Isobel said as she got up and began sorting through a stack of music. "I haven't played it in a long time." Suddenly her hands paused, and she stared at something on the opposite side of the room.

Caleb turned. There, frolicking on the top of the other piano and looking as though they were having a grand time, were all four of Clara's kittens. Dorcas turned around to see what was happening just as the kittens slipped under the lid.

"What are those cats doing in the piano?" Dorcas demanded as she set down her coffee cup with a clink.

Caleb smiled as his two favorite women began fishing kittens out of the piano. Yes, his life was truly blessed.

FOOL ME TWICE

ANNIE JONES

To Molly Fox

ONE

Let's face it—many women dreamed as little girls that they would one day find and marry their prince. Many men expected that when the time came, they'd marry a girl just like the girl who married dear old Dad, their perfect fit, their very own Cinderella—except she'd look like Cindy Crawford, of course."

Ginny Sanborn looked up to acknowledge her classroom full of restless college students. "Then reality came crashing in on that youthful fantasy world, and an awful lot of women found themselves settling for the distant relative of their Prince Charming: The Duke of Doesn't-Scratch-Himself-in-Public."

Snickering, pens scratching over thick pads of notebook paper, and whispered responses answered Ginny's half-jest.

"And a lot of men chose not to 'settle' at all, avoiding commitment in fear that if they chose one girl, the very next day they'd meet their ideal woman, their Cindy-rella-mom."

It was Friday before spring break. Ginny's Sociology of Interpersonal Relationships class was only two-thirds full. She felt that those who had made the effort to show up today when the temptation to skip out early was so great deserved to hear something interesting and applicable to their lives. So today she decided to speak on one of her most passionate subjects—the myth of romantic love.

Ginny tugged at the hem of her fitted blazer, then smoothed her hand up her sleek French twist. She knew that not a single strand of golden hair nor a seam or thread of the blue suit was out of place. The gesture only gave her audience a chance to soak in her statement.

She glanced out the window at the Oklahoma wind-whipped landscape and the familiar setting of the college campus. She was well into her fourth year teaching here, and Phillips University felt as much like an extension of herself as her wire-rimmed reading glasses did.

There had been a time when she had thought of leaving the comfort of her home and the closeness of small-town and university life. She fingered the pink slip of paper with the phone message from the man who had expected her to change her entire life for him but had refused to change even his mule-headed mind for her.

Adam Buckman. Her heart skipped at the thought of the rugged cowboy whom she had dated for three years without the natural progression expected in most relationships, despite his alleged feelings for her. He'd bought himself quite a bit of time with his "I love you's," but in the end they had not been enough. Ginny had needed a more permanent demonstration. She'd needed a commitment.

Adam simply refused to give that to her. A flash of pain slashed through her at that knowledge, even six months after their break-up. If Adam could have lived his love instead of just talking about it, she would not be giving this lecture today.

She glanced down at her notecards but saw only the phone message as she said, "Not all prospects for romantic relationships are this grim, of course." She skimmed one fingertip over her secretary's scrawled note, practically stroking Adam's concise request. *Please call.*

Sure, she thought, her throat constricting as she forced down a surge of unresolved emotion. She'd call, all right.

When it snowed here in Enid, Oklahoma, in August.

"There are many references in the Bible to love, and we've already talked about the different kinds of love noted." Even though Phillips was a Christian university, she did not always put biblical references into her lectures. This time it was warranted. "But have you ever noted that when we find specifics about men and women loving one another, there are two different sets of instructions—one for wives and another for…husbands?"

She almost choked on the word. *Husband.* The one thing she would never have. The one thing Adam would never be.

No, she told herself, adjusting her glasses, she'd made the right choice in deciding not to return Adam's call. She bowed her head, scanning her notes to quell the riot of feelings these pointless thoughts had stirred in her. She mustn't let her lecture suffer by allowing herself to dwell on an impossible relationship.

"Could that be because God knows what we often don't want to acknowledge in modern society?" She gripped the edges of her podium. "That men and women are, in the way they approach this most basic bond, not just from two different worlds but from worlds that seem at the opposite ends of the universe?"

Her hand moved to the pink slip of paper, and in one quick movement she crumpled it inside her fist.

Fool me once, shame on you, but fool me twice, shame on me. That's how the old saying went. She bowed her head for just a moment to refocus her energy and rally her inner strength. Adam Buckman had made a fool of her once by leading her on as he did. She would not give him the chance to do it again.

Wham!

Ginny jumped at the slam of the heavy classroom door a

181

few feet away. At first she refused to dignify the rudeness of the latecomer by acknowledging him or her, and she kept her gaze lowered. Then she gritted her teeth and spoke in her most authoritarian tone, "If you can't be on time for my lectures, at least have the courtesy to be quiet when you do get here."

Was her mind still in the past, or was that the sound of cowboy boots she heard striding toward the platform?

A sense of foreboding sank like a chunk of ice into the pit of her stomach. The scent of leather and bracing aftershave tweaked her nose. The sound of the footsteps halted.

Ginny jerked her head up to catch mischief flickering at her from a pair of all-too-familiar brown eyes.

"Adam," she whispered.

A shudder rippled from high in her chest straight down to her knees. Her pumps skiffed over the linoleum floor as she shuffled backward.

A hush rolled across the classroom.

Adam Buckman touched two fingers to the brim of his dark brown hat and dipped his head. "Howdy, Gin."

"Wh-what are you doing here?" she managed to get out.

"I've come for you, darlin'," he said in that low voice that sounded soothing yet aggressive at the same time.

She tried to swallow. Or blink. Or even breathe. But those most basic instincts eluded her.

Somewhere beyond him, her students became a murmuring blur.

He stepped forward.

The sight of Adam engulfed her. His broad shoulders all but blotted out the classroom behind him. The shocked reaction of her classroom faded from her sight with each inch that Adam closed between them.

Like a pivotal scene in a bad movie, the whole event took

on a surreal quality, as if it were happening in slow motion. He moved near enough for the sharp, citric smell of his aftershave to sting her nostrils.

She slicked her tongue over her parted lips and retreated another step. The heel of her shoe snagged on a nick in the floor. She had to pinch the earpiece of her glasses to hold them in place.

He flashed a grin, his teeth fiercely white in contrast to the dark stubble on his cheeks.

Her heart stopped. It had to have stopped; otherwise she would have been able to do something, to say something. Instead she just stared at the waves of deep brown hair creating a thick fringe over his collar.

A shadowy, day-old beard defined the lines of his strong jaw. His chest rose and fell in a heavy, hypnotic rhythm. She shut her eyes for an instant but could still see his image glimmering behind her closed lids. Adam Buckman was here, so close she could smell his skin, touch his body, kiss him senseless.

Senseless. Now there was an appropriate word for the moment. She moved from behind the safety of the podium, ready to confront her own traitorous feelings and the man who caused them. She drew in her breath.

The sound of boots shifting on the cold floor answered her. Ginny glanced at his face, and from the shade of his low-fitting hat, he winked at her.

Her breath rushed from her lungs in a great whoosh. Still, she got a coherent sentence out for both Adam and her students to hear. "You're disrupting my class, Mr. Buckman."

"That's *Dr.* Buckman, ma'am." He raised his eyebrows at her.

"*Dr.* Buckman," she mimicked, fully aware that some people might think he, a veterinarian, deserved the title more than she. "You're disrupting my class, and I'm going to have to ask you to leave. I simply do not have time to talk to you right now."

"Good," he said, the tilt of his lips echoed by the laughter in his eyes. "Because I didn't come here to talk."

One large hand snatched her by the wrist.

Her stomach lurched. Confusion clashed with excitement within her.

He used her arm to pull her so close she could see the thin film of sweat on his taut neck just inside his open collar. She felt the warmth of his body pressing in on her.

"Really, Adam." She tried to sound aloof, but the crack in her voice betrayed her. "I demand that you tell me what's going on here."

"You," he said in a coarse whisper that was pure Adam and no act. "You, dear Ginny, are going on. On my shoulder."

He bent low and fit his shoulder neatly into her midsection.

She gasped and fell helplessly forward, her feet lifting from the floor. The physical sensation was disconcerting yet exhilarating.

"If you won't give me a few minutes of your time, then I guess I'll just have to steal them," Adam whispered for only her to hear. He clamped his arms over her legs and clutched them tightly to his body.

"Adam, are you insane?" she cried as her hands flailed about trying to find something to hold onto. "I demand you put me down this instant."

"I don't think you're exactly in a position to make demands, darlin'." He chuckled.

"Put me down, I said." Her fist came down to land a soft thud on his broad back.

He laughed at the feeble attack, then turned to face the

class, giving them a less-than-flattering view of their professor.

The brim of his hat rasped against her skirt as he nodded to her students and said, "Pardon the intrusion, folks. Don't worry about Dr. Sanborn; she's in good hands."

Laughter from the class rang in Ginny's ears as she struggled again to right herself. Her heart hammered in her chest. The blood running to her head coupled with the unwelcome thrill of his nearness made it hard to think as she wriggled in Adam's iron grasp.

"Now, if you'll excuse us," Adam addressed her students as though it were the most natural thing in the world to have their teacher slung over his shoulder. "We've got to hit the trail. Class dismissed."

He spun on his boot heel and strode toward the door through the squawk of chairs pushing back, papers shuffling, and chatter.

With considerable effort, Ginny managed to lift her head and nail her students with an icy glare. "Class is most certainly *not* dismissed. Anyone leaving will be counted absent. I'll be right back as soon as I take care of this."

"What are we supposed to do, Dr. Sanborn?" a young man called out from the classroom chaos.

"Should I call for help?" a female student chimed in.

"No thanks, honey," Adam said, swinging the door open. "She's hefty, but it ain't nothing I can't handle."

"Hefty?" Ginny gasped, but she forced herself to find a retort. "That's surprising talk coming from a man who looks all muscle—"

Adam's stiff spine pulled even straighter with pride.

"All muscle from the neck up!" Ginny propped herself up on Adam's taut back and called out to her class, "You-all stay seated. I'll be back in a few minutes to discuss this little demonstration of the wildly differing approaches the sexes take to the bonding ritual."

Then Adam stepped across the threshold and let the heavy door fall shut behind them with a thunderous bang.

TWO

I f your goal, Adam Buckman, was to embarrass me, then congratulations, buddy-boy, you've accomplished it. Now put me down."

"Not so fast, Dr. Sanborn." He wrung her title and name through his teeth slowly, as if squeezing every ounce of propriety from them.

Holding her like this—in fact, just seeing her again—had his heart thumping like the thrashing hooves of a wild bronc. But he didn't dare let Ginny know that, not if he wanted his plan to work, and a man didn't go to this much trouble for a plan *not* to work.

He strode down the deserted hallway with the only woman capable of making him this loco hoisted high on his shoulder. "I can't put you down until you promise not to retaliate."

She writhed in his grasp, trying to jab his chest with her knee.

He wound his arm more tightly across her legs, commanding, "Promise."

She sniffed, indignant.

He came to a stop beside the glass doors that led outside the building. Afternoon sunlight streamed in over both of them, highlighting the plump feminine curves of her body. Suddenly a moving shadow on the floor behind him snagged his attention away.

"Ah, ah, ah," he warned. "I didn't think you were the type

to resort to violence to solve a problem, Gin."

He watched the silhouette of her raised fist until it relaxed and fell limply against his back.

"Now promise you'll behave, and I'll let you down."

"I'll do no such thing."

That figured. Compromise was never this lady's strong suit in the past. But he believed she had it in her, and with the right coaxing...

His chest tightened at the thought of just how he'd like to coax Ginny. Long, slow kisses in front of a blazing fire in his home just outside Tulsa would be nice for starters. Of course, time and circumstances did not allow that at present, so a more aggressive style of attitude enhancement seemed in order. "Looks like I'll have to resort to drastic measures to protect myself from your feminine fury."

"From my—" Her hand flattened to his back. "What are you talking about?"

A bright flash of light answered her question before Adam could. He struck a pose for a second picture, then turned to put Ginny's face to the camera and its owner.

"Billy Owens!" Ginny's tone mixed delight with disbelief. "I should have known you'd be in on this."

"Ma'am." Billy tipped his chocolate brown cowboy hat to her and grinned like a sly bobcat. "You knew the big guy couldn't have pulled off something this asinine all on his lonesome, didn't you?"

Adam chuckled, jostling Ginny to keep a secure grip on her. "As I recall, when we were all in college together at Oklahoma State, I pulled off a lot of things more asinine than this without any help from you, Billy-boy."

"Do yourself a favor, Buckman," Billy said with a laugh. "Quit while you're ahead."

"You can apply that advice double to your manhandling of me," Ginny added with vehemence. She flexed her warm palm over the muscles of his back.

Her touch sent a ripple of gooseflesh down his back, and a shudder rattled him to the pit of his stomach. He had to get her away from him before he lost the presence of mind to carry out his plan. Stiffly, he bent to set her feet on the floor.

"Wait. One more picture," Billy called out.

Ginny protested, "What do you need a picture for?"

"We want a picture that captures more than your posterior for posterity," Adam grumbled, twisting his head to peer at her over the curve of her back.

"Or for the college newspaper," Billy chimed in.

"You wouldn't!" she gasped.

"We might. But we won't if you don't call security and have us thrown off campus. Deal?"

She drew in a deep breath.

Adam gritted his teeth and waited, wanting nothing more than to release her. Or to press her whole body against his in a long-overdue kiss.

In one sigh that captured her pure exasperation, she relented. "Okay, no security. But you don't need another picture. You have one already."

"Not one that shows your face," Billy said. "Now say 'Cheese.'"

"Sleaze," she accused through gritted teeth.

"Close enough." He snapped the photo.

Adam shut his eyes and clenched his teeth as he lowered Ginny to the ground. He didn't know whether he felt more relief from being rid of the weight of her or from being freed of her nearness. He dug his fingers into the aching muscles along his neck. "Have you put on weight? Guess that's what comes from not having a man to chase you around, huh?"

"For your information, I am not the type to allow a man to chase me around, even to keep me in shape." She skimmed both hands down her skirt, then crossed her arms at waist level.

"Does that mean you don't have a man, or you've got one but he won't chase you?" Adam raised an eyebrow.

"It means…" She stopped, then shook her head hard. "What difference does that make? The real question is, what are you doing here, and why did you disrupt my class?"

"He's staying in town all week long," Billy said.

"For spring break?" she asked.

Adam grunted. "There's a whole world beyond this university, Ginny, where not everything is measured in quarters, semesters, and winter and spring breaks, you know."

Ginny blinked. "I…I know."

"Naw, Adam didn't come to Enid for spring break. He came to get fitted for a tux and to move furniture. Not to mention the bachelor party." Billy stepped up and clapped Adam hard on the back.

"Bachelor party?" Her face suddenly went pale as she faced Adam. "You mean you're…you're getting…married?"

Her last word broke into a whisper. Her lower lip trembled. Was it wishful thinking, or did the thought of him marrying another really affect her so?

"Him?" Billy barked out with a sharp laugh. "Who'd marry that old stubborn lunkhead?"

She straightened and rolled her gaze down the length of Adam, as though sizing up a good-for-nothing ranch hand wanting a bonus in his paycheck. Her smile, about as welcoming as a cactus kiss, did not reflect in her eyes. "Yes, who indeed?"

Adam watched her reaction and had to wonder if he had

vastly miscalculated his chances of winning Ginny back. Here they were, away from the prying eyes of her students, and yet Ginny greeted his arrival with more annoyance than interest. Sure, he'd known better than to expect her to fling herself at him, but she could at least seem happy to see him again.

Maybe two months of dreaming of this reunion had caused him to romanticize their whole relationship. Maybe the impending wedding of his best friend had put him in a far too sentimental frame of mind. Maybe he was just a big old mush-headed mule for hoping this demonstration of affection would show her he had changed, that he could now flaunt his emotions for her in front of the whole world.

He folded his arms over his chest. "Billy and Lisa are getting married on Friday, a week from today."

Ginny placed one neatly manicured hand to her cheek. Her green eyes grew wide behind the thin lenses of her glasses. "A week from *today?*"

"It sure is," Billy said with a sappy grin as he tucked his small camera into his shirt pocket.

Adam raised his chin. "I'm the best man."

For the first time since he'd invaded her classroom, she smiled, her eyes sparkling. "You mean *you're* the best man they could get?"

"There's none better, darling," he half growled, his senses suddenly awash with hope again. If he could get her to smile and joke, then maybe…

"I'll bet Lisa would argue with you about that," she teased, not in a mocking voice, but in a sweet, vaguely flirty purr. She turned to Billy. "So, this is it, huh? After all these years, you're finally taking the plunge."

"Right into the deep end." Billy placed his hands together and pantomimed diving. "Which reminds me, I told Lisa I'd meet her in a few minutes, so I gotta scoot. Oh, and Ginny, Lisa asked me to tell you she's looking forward to y'all getting together tomorrow."

"Tomorrow?"

"You know, the bridal shower."

"The shower!" She winced. "I'd completely forgotten it. Luckily, I still have time to get her a gift."

Billy's dark brows angled down over his eyes as he shifted a look from Ginny to Adam to Ginny again. "Don't let me influence you or anything, but I wouldn't complain if you got her something slinky."

"Billy Owens!" Ginny took a step back. "I can't believe you said that."

"He's in love and going to get married in a week, Gin." Adam leaned so close he could see her eyes dilate as he finished in a gruff whisper. "Believe it."

A faint flush brightened her cheeks. "Oh, Adam, really."

"Really." He raised his eyebrows to punctuate the word.

She met his gaze and caught her breath in a quiet gasp that turned the knife of tension tighter in his gut.

Billy pushed the door open, then paused to touch his hat to bid them farewell. "Just another seven days and five hours and we'll be an old married couple off on our honeymoon."

Ginny shifted her attention to Billy and, as subtly as a drowning man grasps for a lifesaver, seized the change of subject. "And where are you going on your honeymoon, Bill?"

The man shrugged and headed out the door, calling back, "Who cares? Ain't like we plan on leaving the room anytime that week."

Ginny swallowed so hard it made Adam wince and do the same.

He cleared his throat to chase away any huskiness as he

showed her some mercy and redirected the conversation in earnest. "I'm sorry about making a scene in the classroom, Gin—"

"Sorry doesn't change anything, Adam. Actions, not empty words, change things."

"I thundered into your room and hauled you off on my shoulder!" He shook his head. "How much more action do you want, girl?"

She glared at him.

"Okay, all joking aside. I was trying to make a point, and I *am* sorry if I used the wrong method." He held out his hand to her. "Apology accepted?"

She glanced at his offered hand, then slowly began to shake her head. "This was our problem all along, your thinking that you could do whatever you wanted—or not do anything at all—as long as you said the right things to appease me."

"But I—"

"Well, never again." She put her hands to her hips. "I don't know what on earth you could say that could make up for your humiliating antics in my classroom today."

"Well, then maybe there's something I can *do.*"

She narrowed her eyes at him. "Pardon me?"

He whisked his black hat from his head and instinctively raked his fingers back through his wavy brown hair. "I said maybe there is something I can do to make up for everything I've put you through."

"I don't understand."

He stepped toward her, his boots echoing in the cool, dim hallway. "That's why I came here today, Ginny. I've done a lot of thinking since we broke up."

She tipped her chin up. "I can only imagine how taxing *that* was for you."

He smiled. "I deserved that, I'm sure."

She didn't contradict him.

"But I also deserve something else from you, Gin."

"What?"

"A second chance."

A second chance? She took one step backward, then stepped back again until her spine pressed rigidly against the unyielding wall. *Fool me once, shame on you...*

"A second chance at what?" she asked.

"At us. At our relationship."

Fool me twice, shame on me.

"Go away, Adam. If I had wanted to see you, I would have returned your call." Her sensible heels skidded easily over the slick floor as she pivoted away from him. "Now if you'll excuse me, I have to find some way to restore order to my class."

"Losing you made me reexamine my priorities, my methods of handling things, my goals in life." He moved directly into her path.

She sidestepped him without missing a beat and continued toward her classroom.

"What are you afraid of, Gin?"

She jerked to a halt. *Everything, you big idiot,* she wanted to cry out. *I'm afraid of everything, afraid of what you make me feel and want, afraid that if I let you near me you'll break my heart again.*

"I'm busy, Adam. I'm in the middle of a lecture you'd do well to listen to."

"I've changed, Ginny. And the way I see it, I have the next week to prove to you just how much."

"Starting with this little stunt, I suppose?"

"You *are* the one who wanted me to do more than just talk about my feelings. You wanted a demonstration."

"Bursting in on my lecture wasn't exactly what I had in mind, Adam."

Or was it? What better way to save face and also prove her point to both Adam and her class than to use a little creative visual aid?

She peered at him over her shoulder. *Why not?* "Are you serious about wanting to find ways to demonstrate how you've changed?"

He strummed his fingers over the brim of the hat in his hands. "The one thing you know about me, Gin, is I don't say a thing unless I mean it."

"Good. Come with me." She motioned for him to follow as she started back toward her classroom.

"What have you got in mind, Gin? You don't plan on dissecting me, do you?"

A wistful smile tugged at her lips at the thought. "No, I don't plan on dissecting you. I plan on using you to save my lecture on male-female relationships."

"I don't know about *that.*" His footsteps slowed. Only someone who had known the man as long as she had could have picked up on the gentle jest in his tone as he asked, "You don't plan on offering me up as a bad example of manhood, do you?"

"I am going to make an example out of you, Adam," she said. "And you may learn something in the process yourself."

"I look forward to it, then." He fit his hat down so low she couldn't help but focus on his deep, calm gaze. "Just what is it I'm to be an example of, by the way?"

"You, Dr. Adam Buckman, are the strong silent type, the stuff of western legends."

His chest puffed up a bit at what he perceived to be a compliment.

Ginny narrowed her eyes and smiled like a kid with a pin ready to prick an overinflated balloon. "You are a walking example of why men and women can never let their hearts rule their minds in matters of romance."

"If that's what it takes," he mumbled, following behind her and finding a seat in the classroom.

"And in conclusion, nothing better illustrates the vast differences in the way men and women communicate emotions than the demonstration so thoughtfully provided by Dr. Buckman." Ginny raised her head, straightened her notecards, and removed her glasses. "If there are no questions, then…"

Hands shot up throughout the room.

"I'll take two or three questions, and then class is dismissed." Ginny gripped the sides of the podium.

Adam leaned forward in the chair he'd taken at the back of the room and studied the woman he hoped to take back to Tulsa as his wife. She had a lot of nervous energy. Always did have. In fact, during their years together, he'd taken great pleasure in teasing her about creative ways to vent that pent-up energy. He'd enjoyed that almost as much as he enjoyed knowing he still spurred that kind of reaction in her.

Ginny's gaze flitted over the room but managed to avoid making eye contact with Adam. She settled on a mousy-haired girl in a dress that looked like it had been stolen from someone's granny and nodded. "You have a question?"

"I have a question." Adam stood.

Heads turned. Chairs shifted.

Ginny slipped her glasses back on and blinked her enormous eyes at him. "Dr. Buckman, this discussion is limited to students of mine."

"I understand that." He placed his hands on his hips.

"That's nice to know." Only the tremble in her hand betrayed any emotion as she whisked back an imaginary stray lock of golden hair. She drew in a deep breath and focused on the granny-girl again, but Adam didn't give either the chance to speak.

"I'm not afraid to admit that over the years we've known one another," he ran his thumb and forefinger along the rim of his black hat and dipped his head to her, "you've taught me a thing or two."

Laughter erupted in the room.

Ginny raised her head and nailed him with a look as steady as any bull about to charge. One fist planted on her hip, she spoke above the students' laughter. "That may well be, Dr. Buckman, but no matter how hard I tried, I don't seem to have taught you a thing about manners."

That-a-gal. Stand up to me. Show me that the old Ginny hasn't been completely swallowed up by this prim schoolmarm with the doesn't-believe-in-love act. "If you're talking about my hat, ma'am—" and he knew good and well she wasn't — "I'd take it off, but there's no place to put it."

"Oh, really?" Her shoes clicked as she rounded the podium, raring for a fight. "Well, may I suggest you take that classic example of a grown man's pathetic need to act out his adolescent bad-boy fantasies and put it…"

Granny-girl gasped.

"…under your seat." Ginny cocked her head and raised one eyebrow.

"Thank you, ma'am, but I think I'll cling to my adolescent fantasies a little while longer, if you don't mind." He hooked his thumbs into his belt loops and lowered his eyelids and his voice. "And I'll keep my hat on, too."

She forced a long blast of air through her clenched teeth.

Adam smiled. "Now about that question, ma'am."

Ginny glanced down at her naked wrist and shook her head. "My, my, look at the time. I think we'd better—"

"Can you really stand there and in good conscience try to convince these people that men and women have such different views, goals, and needs from a relationship that unless they look at it from an objective vantage point they are doomed to difficulties?"

"I'm only teaching what I learned from—" Her gaze locked with his for one moment. She bowed her head and walked to the safety of the podium before finishing. "I'm not teaching anything that my research doesn't support."

"You mean your personal research." In other words, he'd done this to her. And he'd have felt like a first-class jerk about it, too, except that he'd come back now to put everything right. He couldn't afford the luxury of wasting time wallowing in regret. Ginny needed him to show her how he felt, and she needed that now.

He stepped from the row of chairs into the aisle. "I'm afraid your research may be flawed, Dr. Sanborn."

She stepped back. "I don't think it is. And I don't think you can convince me otherwise."

"Even if I say that I've come here this week to sweep you totally off your feet? And that I hope that by the end of this week, you'll not only have forgiven me my hardheaded male mistakes but you'll have agreed to become my wife?"

THREE

The metal hooks of heavy hangers scraped atop their rods, moved along by someone pushing through a too-narrow gap between peignoirs and panties. The illuminated curves of a stocking display wobbled.

Ginny tensed. Even without looking, she realized that slipping into the least likely place on earth to find a cowboy—the women's intimate apparel section of a crowded department store—had not kept Adam from following her.

After class yesterday she had managed to dodge his eager invitation to dinner. She had refused to answer her phone last night or return the messages left on her machine. Adam simply had to learn that making a big fool of himself was not the same as demonstrating his love for her.

Pretty words now did not absolve him of the past. If he had changed, he'd have to prove it over time, not by blurting out some groundless claim. She'd been burned by his words before, and now she needed more than words.

She supposed he thought that was what he was giving her with this dogged display of determination. This morning, when she had hopped into her car and headed out to the town's only shopping mall, she had noticed his gleaming black pickup on her tail.

Ignore him, she had told herself. She'd had six months of practice at not thinking about that man; surely she could get through another week.

Still, she could not so easily blot out the bold proclamation he'd made in her class yesterday. She had gone to sleep hearing his words. He'd said he'd come to sweep her off her feet and to get her to agree to become his wife. Her heart thrashed out a faster and faster rhythm in her chest as those words and his unmistakable presence closed in on her.

Sheer stubborn pride kept her head bowed over the selection of lace and satin on the rack in front of her. She had come here, after all, to pick out a present for Lisa's shower this afternoon, and she would not let Adam distract her from even one more of her responsibilities.

She pulled a purple satin, black-feather-trimmed teddy from the rack and held it up. A pair of melt-your-heart brown eyes met her gaze just above the deep v of the neckline.

"Nice," he said.

She shoved the garment back onto the rack so fast the hangers clattered, and other flimsy pieces fluttered in flashes of silk and lace. She felt the sting of a blush on her cheeks, neck, even the tip of her nose. Still, she held her composure as tightly and neatly as the French braid at the back of her head.

"Why, Adam Buckman. Imagine seeing you in women's lingerie."

Whether it was her calm or her remark that knocked the smirk right off his face, Ginny didn't know, and she didn't care. She just turned her back and made a show of interest in a rack of chiffon-and-lace nighties. "Really, Adam, following me here is too much. I told you I didn't want to spend time with you while you're here for the wedding. Can't you take no for an answer?"

"Not unless no is the answer I want to hear."

She felt his gaze, but she could not meet it. "You're the last person who should be lecturing someone about getting the answer they want to hear."

"I don't think I've strung together enough words in my entire lifetime to make a lecture." Strain underscored the jest. "That's your department."

"Bringing up yesterday's disastrous lecture situation is hardly the way to ingratiate yourself to me."

"Even if I promise to remove my adolescent fantasy symbol as I do?" He straightened and whisked two fingers along the brim of his black Stetson.

She rolled her eyes and toyed with the top button on her starched white blouse. "I guess I should apologize for making that remark in class. I know you have every legitimate cause to have a trusty black Stetson, and I shouldn't have impugned your reasons for wearing it."

"Well, you know how a cowboy feels about his hat, ma'am." He adjusted it lower on his head, unwittingly emphasizing the deep, hungry look in his warm eyes. "It's second only to his horse and his woman in his heart."

"In that order?" she murmured.

"You know better than that."

"Do I?" She folded her arms over her chest. "I guess if I did, we wouldn't be standing in a public department store arguing."

"We're not arguing, are we, Ginny?"

She put one hand up. "No, you're right. We're not. I'm shopping, and you're leaving."

She pivoted on her heel and focused every ounce of her attention on the rack of silky nightgowns before her.

"You're making this very difficult for me, you know."

"*I'm* not doing anything but shopping for a gift." She pulled out a sheer pink gown. It shimmied with a telltale tremor of her hand. "If this is difficult for you, you have no one but your-self to blame."

Adam opened his mouth to say something, but just then a small woman with steel blue hair and a designer suit approached them. "May I help you?"

"No, thank—"

"We're looking for something special, ma'am." Adam spoke to the salesclerk, but his gaze never wandered from Ginny's face. "It's for a honeymoon."

Honeymoon. Despite her anger, the very notion of a honey-moon with Adam made Ginny's breath catch in the back of her throat.

"Oh, how delightful. When is the big day?"

"Oh no." Ginny shook her head, slammed back into reality by the question. "It's not—"

"Soon, I hope," Adam said, cutting off her explanation.

"Soon?" The salesclerk's pencil-thin brows rose in surprise.

"This is a gift *for a friend.*" Ginny hammered home the last words to make herself perfectly clear. "I think this will do nicely, thank you."

There, she thought as she handed the chosen gown to the clerk. That was that. She'd made her selection; now she could get out of here. Alone.

Throwing her shoulders back with more dignity than she really felt, she marched to the sales counter, trying not to notice the huge cowboy-shaped shadow at her heels.

Every sound from the cash register grated on Ginny's nerves. The growling rip of her check being torn from the book, the crackle of the receipt, even the voices of busy shop-pers all around them ruffled her already agitated state. No wonder her tone came out harsh and impatient when she flat-tened her hand on the gown to keep the clerk from sliding it into a bag and said, "Can I get this gift wrapped?"

"Yes, certainly, dear. But it will take a while," came the reply. "If you have some more shopping to do in the mall or want to go get some lunch—"

"Now there's an idea." Adam curved his hand around Ginny's arm.

At his touch, every muscle in her body tightened. Her thoughts flew back to the incident in her classroom and her unceremonious ride on this man's shoulder. She glanced around at the sedate setting. Enid was not a tiny town, but it was small enough that in any given place—and most especially at Oakwood Mall—there was someone you knew around or, at the very least, someone who knew someone you knew.

Ginny gulped. She simply could not have a repeat of yesterday's indignity here. All her senses went on full alert.

"C'mon, Gin." Adam's fingers wound around her upper arm. "Let's get some lunch; then we can come back for the present."

"Lunch?" She jerked her arm away, seizing the first thing that came to mind to fend off any further contact. "I'm surprised you'd even suggest it, considering how fat you think I've grown since we broke up."

"Fat? I never said that." His expression told her he honestly did not know what she meant. "You look great to me, Ginny. And if you took anything I said yesterday to mean otherwise, I am truly sorry."

He looked and sounded sorry. But Ginny felt that this tack was her only defense mechanism to keep him at bay physically and emotionally. That revelation hit her hard.

Had she really softened enough toward Adam that she needed contrived annoyance at a nonissue to keep from letting her guard down around him? Her near panic at the grain of truth in that thought edged her tone louder as she adjusted her glasses and said, "You say you're sorry now, Adam, but what does that change? It doesn't erase the things you've done. It doesn't give me back all the wasted time I spent waiting for you to decide you wanted to make a life with me. It doesn't make me—"

She cut herself off, her hand pressing hard against her chest. Here she'd thought to stop him from making a scene in public, and then she had gone and shouted out her frustrations for everyone to hear.

"I get the feeling we aren't talking about my clumsy jokes about your weight anymore, are we?"

She bit her lip and shook her head, well aware that gazes from every direction in the store remained riveted on her.

"Maybe we should talk about it." He offered her his arm. "Over lunch?"

She swallowed hard—she had to swallow hard to push down her last shred of pride—and accepted his arm.

"All right. I'll go to lunch with you, Adam." She collected the receipt she'd need to reclaim Lisa's wrapped present and lifted her head high. She paid no attention to the gawks and smiles of the other shoppers until she and Adam reached the store's outside door. Only then did she steal a quick peek to see that no one still watched them.

She dropped his arm, her chin, and her voice to let him know that he may have won the battle, but she was still at war. "I'll go to lunch with you, Adam. I'll even offer to pick up the check since I plan to decide where we'll be eating. But there's one thing you should know."

"What's that?"

"All the *talking* in the world won't make any difference. I have no intention of letting you break my heart again."

~ ~ ~ ~ ~

He should never have let Ginny pick the place for them to share their lunch. But she had demanded they take their separate vehicles, asking him to follow her. She led him to a fast-food drive through, then down a back road alongside the mall, and farther still until they stopped near the edge of town.

Adam stared at the hamburger and french fries on rumpled paper atop a badly weathered picnic table. Even with his back to the fenced-off airfield of Vance Air Force Base, he was still keenly aware each time a jet took off or landed.

"There are plenty of nice restaurants around town, Ginny. Even more than one park we could have gone to, if you insisted we eat outdoors. Why did you have to choose a roadside table beside a busy runway?"

She shrugged and smiled from behind her raised hamburger. "It's close to the mall. I still have to go back there and pick up Lisa's gift, you know. It just seemed like the most convenient spot."

"Yeah, convenience." He snorted. "I suspected that's exactly what brought us to a place this noisy and distracting when I wanted to have a serious talk with you."

"What was that?" She put her hand to her ear.

"I said—" The whine of a jet engine blistered his ears.

She sat there, all smiles, showing no distress at the nerve-racking sound.

The glaring late-March sun reflected off the aircraft over his shoulder and the still yellow grass all around them, stinging Adam's eyes despite the shade of his hat. The wind had quick-cooled the food until it was distinguishable more by shape and texture than by its flat taste. None of the discomfort mattered, of course, if it afforded him another chance to reach his Ginny, to make her understand she meant the world to him.

He stretched his arm across the battered tabletop to take her hand in his. She drew her hand back until only her chilly fingers remained in his grasp.

The jet engine growled louder.

Adam winced but would not be deterred. "Clearly, you don't want to hear what I have to say, but you can't stop me from saying it, Ginny."

The set of her jaw, the spark in the depths of her lovely eyes, the way she churned her plastic straw in the crushed ice of her soda all told him she had heard him.

"What do I have to do to convince you of my feelings, Ginny? Of my sincerity? Just tell me, and I'll do it."

The wind whipped through the shaded area, but not a single hair on her head ruffled. She fixed a gaze on him almost as unyielding as her tight braid.

Low in his gut he felt a wrenching at her response, but he had to press on. "I love you, Ginny. Our being apart these last few months proved to me just how much. I want us to be married. I thought you wanted the same thing."

"When?"

His brow pushed down. "Six months ago, that's when. You broke up with me because I was taking so long to make the commitment."

Behind him another plane roared to life, forcing him to shout. "Some of my friends told me it was a gamble, a tried-and-true woman's trick to force the marriage issue. Well, your gamble paid off, Ginny, and here I am."

She rose slowly from her side of the picnic table, her face pale. "I meant *when* did you want to get married. Not because I was thinking of doing it, but to see if you could actually name a date."

"Name a date? Gin, I'm ready—honest, I am." He stood,

too, disregarding the food now entirely cold on the table. "*You* name the date."

"All right, I will." She leaned forward, bracing both arms, her palms flat against the splintered wood of the table. "I'll tell you precisely when I'm going to marry you, Adam. Never, that's when!"

She struggled to extract herself with some shred of dignity from the bench seat. When she succeeded, she pivoted, her braid slapping the back of her neck as she did.

Adam clenched his teeth. "Why are you doing this, Ginny?"

"Doing what?" She twisted her head to look over her shoulder and blinked at him.

He strode the few feet to her side. "Acting so stubborn and unwilling to compromise—to even listen to me, much less allow yourself to be open to the idea of our marrying."

"Stubborn? Unwilling to compromise?" She laced her arms over her chest, her eyes shooting little darts of accusation. "Why is it that six months ago when *you* didn't want to marry *me* you were just being cautious and levelheaded, but now that the tables are turned and *I* don't want to marry *you*, I'm stubborn and unwilling to compromise?"

"I never said I didn't want to marry you six months ago," he corrected as gently as the surrounding noise would allow.

"You didn't?" For the first time her features softened toward him.

"I just said we should wait until the time was right."

"In other words, until *you* were good and ready." She rolled her eyes. "And now that *that* time has finally come, I guess I'm supposed to jump at the chance to be your wife?"

He started to say something but stopped. He realized that whatever he managed to sputter out right now would only be used against him, so he clamped his mouth shut again.

"The only place I'm jumping, mister, is back in my car. I still have to pick up my gift and get ready for the shower this afternoon." She walked stiff backed to her car.

"And what am I supposed to do?"

"Well, for starters, you can clear away our lunch trash. Then after that, may I suggest a little Bible study? Start with 1 Peter, chapter 3, verse 7. I referenced it in my lecture yesterday." She put one hand to her eyes to shade them, standing beside her modest little car, all prim and proper.

Maybe he was some kind of fool to think it, but he felt she was giving him some hope, some direction. And he needed whatever direction she could offer. That gave his squashed spirits, if not his ego, a lift.

Those spirits buoyed even higher when she let a bit of playfulness slip into her tone as she added, "Oh, wait, I made the Bible references before you made your entrance."

"So, if I read this passage, will it give me some clue as to what I'm doing wrong with you, Gin?" He put his hands on his hips.

"It should help." She opened the driver's door and started to get inside, then stopped and popped her head up again. "But, Adam?"

"What, Gin?"

"If the verses don't paint the whole picture, maybe you should try listening to a little old Aretha Franklin. You want to know what a woman wants from a man, what I need from you before I can even imagine patching things up with you, much less make a lifetime commitment? First Peter outlines it, and Aretha spells it right out for you."

FOUR

Oooohhh." Billy's fiancée, Lisa, drew a long silk robe from a white gift box. "How perfect! Just like something I've seen in the movies!"

"Did you get that?" Lisa's future mother-in-law whispered to Ginny.

"Got it," she said, dutifully writing down what Lisa had said according to her assignment from the shower's host, Lisa's aunt.

"Okay, that's the last of the presents, ladies." Lisa's Aunt Pat clapped her hands together to get everyone's attention.

Aunt Pat, as everyone who knew her called the woman, shared her elderly years with Aunt Nana, her sister-in-law. Some said the two were a few noodles short of a casserole, and no one argued that their home was about three cats over minimum health standards. But generally they were, as one native to the area had observed, "a hoot."

"Bow Lady? Bow Lady?" Aunt Pat placed one hand to the side of her mouth and called out. "Where are you, Bow Lady?"

"Here I am!" Aunt Nana sang out in an operatic voice. She floated into the room waving a paper plate with all the ribbons and bows from Lisa's gifts taped to it.

"Oh, Nana, what have you done now?"

"I made a hat, like you told me to," she proclaimed, showing the riot of color to the gathering of women seated on the couch and folding chairs.

"You were supposed to make a ribbon *bouquet*." Aunt Pat

sighed to make sure everyone in the room understood her everlasting frustration.

Ginny thought to use this moment to slip quietly away. She tried to hand the notepad she'd used to record Lisa's responses to the woman seated to her right. No luck.

"Who ever heard of a ribbon bouquet?" Aunt Nana demanded of Aunt Pat.

"Listen to it, Nana, *bow*-quet. It just makes sense. Who ever heard of a ribbon hat?"

"I have. Haven't you ever heard of a *bow*-ler?" Aunt Nana rolled out a deep, contagious laugh.

Ginny turned to the woman on her left, Lisa's future mother-in-law. She thrust the pad toward the woman. "This has been fun, but I have to—"

Aunt Nana swept past just then, knocking into Ginny on her way to plunk her weird creation on Lisa's head.

"Now, where's our note taker?"

Ginny cringed. It was just a little cringe but one she suspected those seated near her saw. To save face, she felt she had to stay and play along. Sneaking out now would be the height of rudeness.

"You there, with the glasses." Aunt Pat pointed right at Ginny. "Madam Professor, isn't it?"

Not to mention impossible. Ginny opened her mouth to speak but never got the chance.

"We're going to recount for everyone a few details of the love story of Lisa and Billy," Aunt Pat announced. "When Nana points to you, Madam Professor, you go down the list of things you've written and read what Lisa said when she opened her gifts. But skip any repeats or just simple thank-yous. Got that?"

Everyone in the room focused on Ginny. She squirmed in the hard folding chair. "Got it."

Aunt Pat waved her arms as she spoke, making sure everyone followed along as she told a little bit about how much everyone loved the engaged couple and then told the real story of how they met and fell in love.

Maybe it was the romantic mood of the afternoon or the fact that Adam had suddenly charged back into her life, but Ginny couldn't help thinking back over her own love story as the woman spoke. She'd been so enthralled by Adam, by his larger-than-life good humor, his dedication to making his new veterinary practice thrive, and his deep-seated faith. Those feelings had not died with time, not even with the break-up. But he had been unable to commit, and she had been unable to keep living with the sense that she was the last priority of his life. If that had truly changed now...

Aunt Pat summed up her story, then turned the floor over to Aunt Nana, who launched full steam into the shower game.

"Of course, you've all heard of love at first sight," Nana said. "But when Lisa laid eyes on her Billy for the very first time, she told everyone within earshot—"

She cued Ginny with a flourish.

"Um—" Ginny glanced down at her notes. "She said, 'I can't wait to get some use out of that.'"

The group laughed.

Ginny recalled the first time she saw Adam. She'd spent the summer at a church camp as a counselor. One day she found an injured dog by the camp's front gate, and the camp director told her who to call for help. Ginny had marveled that the vet could understand the problem over the phone through her sniffles and repeated worry that the sweet dog would not make it.

Adam had driven out immediately and tended to the animal with Ginny acting as assistant. She could still see the summer sun on his broad back. She recalled the way her stomach fluttered at the compelling mix of cowboy brawn and extreme tenderness he showed in treating the scared, injured dog. She knew then that despite his sometimes monumental macho persona, he was a very special, very kind, man.

"Then, when Billy first asked Lisa out on a date, all she could say was—"

Ginny snapped back to the present, wet her lips, and read eagerly, "'Terrific! Another of these and I'll have a different one for every day of the week!'"

Adam, Ginny remembered even as she put on a cheery face for the group, had asked her out the very day they'd met. And she'd accepted.

"The first time Billy ever stole a kiss, our Lisa cried out—"

"'Thank you! Thank you! It's just what I wanted. You read my mind.'" Ginny surprised herself with her own enthusiastic rendition of Lisa's comments.

Maybe that's because she couldn't help thinking of the first kiss she had shared with Adam on a summer night in the Oklahoma countryside with just about a billion of God's gorgeous stars shining down on them.

"Now, if this tradition holds true," Aunt Nana surmised, her round face beaming, "it won't be difficult to predict what Lisa will say to Billy on their honeymoon."

There was that word again, Ginny thought. That big event that she and Adam might never share. She and Adam as honeymooners, imagine that!

"When they're all alone," Nana purred.

She *could* imagine it.

"As he holds her close for the very first time as man and wife, she'll tell him exactly what she's thinking when she whispers—"

"'Oooohhh. How perfect! Just like something I've seen in the movies!'" Even as she got the words out, Ginny felt the tinge of blush on her cheeks. Of course, only she knew that the heat tinging her face came from her own thoughts of being alone with Adam, not from the silly game.

Around her, however, the group joked and teased.

"Why, Ginny," Lisa said, "I do believe you're blushing!"

Ginny hammed it up with a phony look of chagrin at her own response. "What can I say? I guess I'm just one of those icy academics—easily shocked, easily embarrassed."

"Embarrassed? You?" Lisa sputtered out a disbelieving huff. "After what happened Friday, I didn't think anything could embarrass you!"

Ginny's heart sank as the guests scooted to the edges of their seats, murmuring, "What? What happened Friday? Tell us, Lisa."

Ginny felt like dissolving into the floor when Lisa relayed the story, obviously secondhand from Billy, to the entire shower gathering.

The women surrounding Ginny giggled and gasped.

"How romantic!"

"Can you believe it?"

"What would you do?"

"And he ended the whole thing," Lisa said above the hubbub, her expression that of one totally in the know, "with a marriage proposal, right there, in front of the entire class!"

Someone squealed in delight. Someone else clapped her hands.

Ginny pursed her lips, her head shaking as she hurried to issue a correction. "It wasn't actually a proposal. Not technically."

"Then what was it?" Aunt Pat demanded, as if she were the

only one sensible enough to sort the whole situation out. "Just what did he say?"

"Well, he said that he wanted to sweep me off my feet." Ginny pushed her glasses up by touching her fingers to the nosepiece. "And that he wanted me to forgive him for all his mistakes and agree to be his wife."

"Sounds like a marriage proposal to me!" Aunt Nana announced. "You *are* going to accept, aren't you?"

Accept? Until now, Ginny hadn't really given the prospect serious thought. She'd been too angry. But as she recalled her relationship with Adam and remembered the man beneath the black-hat image, her heart filled with hope and excitement. "Well, I..."

"Oh, c'mon, Ginny." Lisa gave her arm a gentle shove. "The man put his big old cowboy ego on the line. He's actively pursuing you and is obviously willing to do whatever it takes to win you back."

That remains to be seen, Ginny thought. But if Lisa's observation did prove true, if Adam was willing to do whatever it took to win her, she might just be won over to his way of thinking as well.

Lisa grinned at Ginny, giving her a friendly nudge. "Honestly, now, how could you *not* marry a man like that?"

"Oh, I never said I wasn't going to marry him," Ginny confessed, her smile shining through for the first time in a long time. "But only if and when he proves to me he's learned a few very important lessons."

Husbands, in the same way be considerate as you live with your wives, and treat them with respect as the weaker partner and as heirs with you of the gracious gift of life, so that nothing will hinder your prayers.

His answer was in that verse. Adam rubbed his eyes and tucked the small pocket-sized edition of the New Testament into the glove compartment of his truck. A grateful farmer had given him the leather copy with Adam's name stamped on it in small gold letters. Since his work often demanded he get into mud and muck and all manner of things, he did not carry the gift in a pocket but kept it always in his truck for reference.

It had come in very handy today as he'd waited in his truck outside the tuxedo rental shop. Billy and the other groomsmen were supposed to meet him there to get measured for their tuxes at one o'clock, but since Adam's lunch date had ended early—and miserably—he had come on ahead. He made use of the time by looking up 1 Peter, chapter 3, as Ginny had suggested.

Adam read the whole of the chapter starting with the admonition to wives. He noted, as had Ginny in her lecture, that these Scriptures came in pairs, with one recommendation to men and another to women. The God who created us obviously knew better than we ourselves did when it came down to relationships.

The glove compartment snapped firmly shut, and Adam leaned back against the sun-warmed upholstery of his truck. Neither the small store nor the streets around it were busy, and the quiet only forced Adam deeper into his own thoughts. Thoughts of Ginny.

He'd forgotten until he'd laid eyes on her again yesterday what a contradiction she could be. All harsh and businesslike on the outside, with proper clothes and her hair arranged to such perfection that one might not suspect how soft and naturally wavy it really was.

But Adam remembered. He remembered the feel of her hair like silk through his fingers and the warm softness of her skin. He remembered the gentle spirit that hid beneath the outward severity and the tender soul that anyone might see if they looked past the glasses perched on her nose and into the depths of her wonderful eyes.

He'd seen it the very first day they'd met, when she'd called his practice, sobbing about a wounded dog near the church camp where she worked that summer. There she'd stood by the side of the road in a camp T-shirt two sizes too big and her hair a wild mess from the wind. From the first time he saw her, he'd known. She was the woman for him.

She had only confirmed that to him when she helped him care for the mutt, then dutifully found the dog's owners even before he returned that night to pick her up for their first date.

He smiled to himself. They dated every night that summer and made plans for their relationship to continue when she went back to her teaching job in Enid. They'd talked of marriage on the last night before they'd parted that summer, and Adam thought she understood that he wanted to postpone the big event until after he'd established his practice. He did not want either his work or his family to suffer because he did not have time to devote himself enough to both.

They had maintained a terrific long-distance relationship. At least he thought it had been terrific, until the last few months before they broke up.

Then suddenly Ginny lost all patience with his need to wait. He shook his head and in doing so caught a glimpse of his own eyes in the rearview mirror.

"Who are you kidding?" he growled to his own image. "There was nothing sudden about it."

He'd known, if he admitted it to himself, that the show-down was on its way for quite a while. Still, he thought that if he could hold off through breeding season, he'd find the time to start his marriage properly. But breeding season turned into birthing season, then preparations for livestock fairs, then getting ready for winter, and then...

And then Ginny had had enough.

Adam pounded his fist against the steering wheel and looked into the blinding glare of the sunlight glinting off the truck's hood. It stung his eyes, but that was nothing compared to the throbbing ache in his chest.

If these last few months without Ginny had taught him anything it was that he'd had a lot more time than he'd ever realized—long, lonely hours from dinner time until he made himself go to sleep, Saturday afternoons, Sunday mornings after church. And he'd spent most of that time missing Ginny.

Now he was ready to make the commitment, to *make* the time so that their relationship and marriage would work. If only he knew what to do to bring Ginny around.

His thoughts went back to the verse Ginny had recommended: *Be considerate.* The phrase rattled through Adam's mind and made him wince at his own behavior. "Considerate!" He huffed. Barging in on Gin's lecture and hauling her out like that. No wonder she would hardly speak to him. What he'd thought a grand romantic gesture, the kind of show of commitment he thought she'd wanted, had been the exact opposite.

He squinted out at the quiet buildings around him and spotted a small, neat little florist just across the way. He'd been a top-notch jerk up until now, first in the way he'd neglected Ginny's feelings and now in the way he'd tried to woo her again.

Well, that was about to change. If Ginny wanted a considerate man for a husband, then he'd become the most considerate cowboy that ever tipped his hat to a lady.

FIVE

G inny found herself singing Aretha Franklin songs as she leaned over to take a big, long whiff of the gorgeous flowers Adam had sent yesterday with, of all things, a hand-written apology.

"I'm sorry I disrupted your class and acted in general like a knuckle-dragging macho moron. Can you forgive me?" she read again.

"I can and I will forgive you, Adam Buckman, *if* this is an indication of things to come. And I mean the apology, not the flowers." She brushed her thumb along the velvety petal of one perfect rose and drew in the mellow fragrance of the arrangement. "Not that I mind the flowers, of course."

She smiled, wondering what Adam would think if he knew his gesture had lightened her mood enough to get her talking and even singing to herself.

A sharp rap at her front door told her that Adam was a few minutes early. Her heels clicked on the highly polished hardwood floor as she rushed to the mirror over the fireplace. Ginny didn't know which of them had been more surprised when she had accepted his offer for a ride to church this morning and lunch after. Well, she argued in silence, she *had* issued the man a challenge to show he had changed. At the very least she owed him the opportunity to prove to her he had.

At the second knock, she pushed at the smooth French twist at the back of her head and pulled free a few wispy curls here and there to frame her face. Then she swept the back of her hand down her pink suit's lapel, calling out, "I'll be there in a minute, Adam."

She rushed to the door, stopped, took a deep breath, and concentrated on keeping a pleasant but detached expression on her face.

"Hello, Adam." The door swinging inward blessedly fanned her in the heat of her excitement. "You're just a bit earl—" She looked out the door and blinked. "Adam, where is your truck?"

The morning sun shimmered over a dark blue sedan in her driveway. She glanced from the car to Adam and gave a tiny gasp.

"And where is your hat?"

He said nothing, just grinned down at her like the cat who ate the canary.

"All right." She plunked her hands on her hips and narrowed one eye. "Who are you and what have you done with Adam Buckman, the pickup-driving, Stetson-wearing, throwing-women-over-his-shoulder, cowboy vet?"

Adam laughed aloud.

But even as she slid into the car he explained he'd borrowed to make her "more comfortable than riding in the pickup," she had to wonder if maybe her urging had changed the man into someone she would no longer recognize.

"If you don't mind, Ginny, since you chose where we ate yesterday, I think I'll pick a place today." Adam glanced across the car to give her a wink.

"Please do." She gave a stiff nod.

He started the car, then twisted around to check behind them before backing out. Streams of churchgoers blocked his path for a moment, so he used the time to study Ginny, sitting prim and proper in the bucket seat beside his.

There was a new softness about her, he decided, nothing he could pinpoint, but something had smoothed down the hard edges of her perpetually ruffled feathers around him. He smiled to himself, thinking, *It had to be the flowers.* He'd gotten it right this time.

She sat in silence, her hands curling the Sunday bulletin into a tight tube.

Still, there was a sense of reserve he thought they would have moved past by now, especially when she agreed to accompany him to church and out to lunch.

She tapped the rolled bulletin against the side of the door, her gaze fixed ahead.

Definitely reserved. He wanted to ask her if he'd assumed too much or perhaps been inconsiderate in some way he did not realize. Instead, he said, "Of course, I'd like your suggestions about where to eat. You probably have a much better idea about what is or isn't crowded on a Sunday."

"You sound like it's been years since you were in town on a Sunday." She cocked her head, her eyes narrowed.

She hadn't worn her glasses this morning. If she were acting any less prickly toward him, he might have suspected she kept them off for his sake, both to look pretty and to have an excuse to stand close to him as they sang from the hymnal. She did look pretty, Adam thought, with or without glasses.

Of course, she'd look prettier if she'd just lighten up and smile at him, he thought.

"Well, it has been a good six months since I've made the Sunday lunch scene in Enid." He eased the car backward, then guided it slowly into the line of cars departing the parking lot. "Things change."

"Yes, they most certainly do, but not that much. Not in that short of a time." Accusation rang in her tone.

He got the idea they weren't talking about places to eat on Sunday, but he played along. "You mean things don't change that much in that short of a time in a town like Enid?"

"Oh, Enid has changed," she said. She settled in her seat and leaned back. "Enid has changed tremendously since I was a girl here. For instance, when I was younger, Mom and Dad would take us kids out to eat after church at the Holland House Buffet. We'd listen to the folks talk, and we'd fill up on fried chicken and potatoes and chocolate pudding. Then we'd all go home and get into our comfortable clothes and enjoy a quiet Sunday."

"Sounds nice." He guided the car out of the Central Christian Church parking lot onto West Main Street.

"It was," she murmured, gazing out the window.

It wasn't hard to imagine the peaceful Sundays of Ginny's childhood as they drove down the residential street under a green canopy of old trees. Large old homes lined their way and spoke of a kind of tranquillity of small-town life that he supposed he rarely experienced anymore living on the edge of Tulsa.

Suddenly it dawned on him that if he and Ginny were to work things out, he would be asking her to leave the life she had always known. As he pulled up to a stop sign, he frowned and turned to her.

"I guess it would be hard for you to ever leave Enid, your family, your friends, your work, your memories."

"Well, I think I could bring my *memories* with me." The warmth of her genuine smile gave Adam renewed hope.

"But it would be hard to leave?"

"Not really. Not for the right reasons."

"Or the right man?"

She looked at him and said nothing.

A car rolled up behind them, and Adam had to move on. "So, you want to go to this Holland House place?"

She shut her eyes. "It isn't open anymore. And that wasn't the point of my telling you about it, Adam."

"I knew it," he muttered. Not for the first time in their relationship, he and Ginny were talking about one thing while she meant something altogether different. "Well?"

She twisted the bright white bulletin in her hands tighter and tighter. She started to speak, then closed her mouth, her jaw clenching.

Adam swerved gently to the side of the narrow street and parked. He cut the engine and positioned himself to face her. The fabric of his good suit chafed the upholstery in the tense silence between them.

"So, Ginny." There was a rasp in his voice. "What *was* your point?"

"That things do change, Adam. Certainly they do." She placed the bulletin in her lap and folded her hands. "The seasons, the places around us, the way we spend our time, they all change. But the things that matter don't fade away or totally transform. Family, home, who we are inside, God's presence in our lives, those essential things remain."

"Why do I have the feeling we're not talking about Enid?"

She broke into a hesitant grin. "I'm just trying to let you know that I never meant for you to reinvent yourself for me. I wouldn't ask that of you."

"I wouldn't ask it of you, either. I respect you too much for that, Ginny, and I love who you are, just as you are, with the possible exception of your stubborn refusal to give in to my cowboy charm and agree to marry me immediately." Adam watched Ginny's reaction to his words. It appeared to be exactly what she wanted to hear, and he meant every bit of it.

"I have changed, Gin," he assured her for good measure.

"I really think you have, Adam. Your apology note went a long way toward convincing me how much."

"As for this car and me showing up on your doorstep 'top-less'—" he pointed to his hatless head— "well, I just wanted to illustrate to you how far I'd go to be the man you need me to be as your husband."

She shifted in the seat, putting her back to the door. "Did you ever stop to think, Adam, that if you just worked on being the man God needs you to be you'd be more than acceptable husband material for any woman?"

"I read that verse you suggested. It gave me something to think about, something to act on."

"I can tell." Sunlight shone over her pale hair.

"I only wish I had more time to spend with you this week, to show you that I am learning."

She stretched her hand out but did not quite touch his arm. "I thought you'd be in town all week."

"It's true I took the week off, but I won't be in Enid the whole time." Suddenly he regretted the plans he'd made half out of friendship, half as a backup plan to keep him from running into Ginny too often if she decided not to give him his second chance. "I promised Billy I'd help him move. He rented a fourteen-foot truck, and we're driving down to Oklahoma City tomorrow to pick up a bedroom suite his grandmother is giving him."

"But that's just one day."

"Actually, we're staying in the city to catch up with some friends from college. Then we'll stay long enough to pick up Billy's cousin who's flying in for the wedding. We won't be back in Enid until late Wednesday."

"Oh." Disappointment clouded her eyes.

"Then on Thursday a bunch of us are helping Lisa and Billy move their stuff into their new house."

The clouds broke, and her face brightened. "I don't suppose they could use another pair of hands to help, could they?"

"Are you kidding?" He knew he was grinning like a wolf in a chicken coop, but he couldn't contain it. This offer meant Ginny wanted to find a way to spend more time with him. "I'm sure Lisa and Billy would love to have your help."

"Good. I'll call Lisa and let her know."

"And until then, we have the rest of today to spend with each other." He rubbed his hands together like a rich man contemplating his wealth. "Starting with lunch."

"So does this also mean you'll respect my recommendations for a place to eat?" She folded her arms over the front of her delicate pink suit.

He ran one hand back to loosen his smoothed-down hair and growled, "As long as it involves steak and potatoes or anything smothered in hot salsa, I'm listening."

"Now, that's the Adam I know and—"

Love? She didn't say it, but his heart filled in the blank for her.

"Appreciate," she finished.

He felt let down, but, gazing into her now relaxed and twinkling eyes, not *too* let down. He reached out to stroke her cheek, uncertain at first if she would pull away.

When she tilted her face into his caress, he let out a long breath he hadn't realized he'd been holding. His gaze dipped to her parted lips.

She wet them in an entirely innocent and unconscious gesture.

Adam's response came without conscious effort as well, but he could not classify it as innocent.

It had been so long since he had kissed Ginny. Really kissed her. Eyes closed. Senses open to the unbelievable softness of her hair, the warmth of her skin, the scent of her perfume.

He half expected her to push him away, but when she wound her fingers around his neck and kissed him back, he lost himself in the moment. When decency demanded that he end the kiss, he moved back fully into his seat and let out a long, low breath.

She cast her gaze downward, a pinkish tinge on her cheek.

Adam smiled as he tipped her chin up and angled it so that he could look into her eyes again and ask, "Does this mean we're making some progress?"

"Yes." She smiled, too. "I do believe it does."

SIX

L ooking for someone?"

Ginny jumped as she let the curtain fall back across Lisa's kitchen window. Ginny had come over to Lisa and Billy's future home early Thursday morning to help with cleaning and preparations for the furniture. "I...um...it's just that, Adam was awfully tired when he called last night, and since he needed his rest so he could work today, I didn't get to see him, and—"

"And you can't wait to throw yourself into his loving arms again," Lisa finished for her.

"Well, I—"

Lisa shook her head, a knowing expression on her face. "You just let me know if you need any motion-sickness pills, girl."

"Motion sickness? What for?"

"For that wild ride you're on." Lisa broke into an impish grin. "Less than a week ago he carted you off on his shoulder and you loathed him, last Saturday you were talking about teaching him a lesson, and today—"

"Today I am simply looking forward to seeing the man again. After all, we shared a very nice Sunday together, lunch and a matinee, a stroll around campus."

"A good-night kiss?"

"No."

"Really?"

A smile eased over Ginny's lips. Her ponytail bounced behind her head as she ducked her chin and admitted, "We didn't wait until night."

"Yep, talk about your wild rides." Lisa laughed. "I just want to know what changed."

"Adam did." Ginny wadded up the hem of her oversize T-shirt in one fist. "Or at least I hope he did."

"He sure seems like the same guy to me."

"Oh, he's basically the same Adam, the same man I fell in love with, but it's how he treats me that's different."

"How's that?"

"With respect. Not that he didn't *act* respectful before," she rushed to add. "But he didn't really respect my feelings before. Otherwise he would never have put off making a commitment for so long."

"So now he's ready to make a commitment?"

"Oh, it's not just that. He seems to be trying to appreciate my point of view in all this. I can't tell you how much that means to me."

Lisa smiled and put her hand on Ginny's shoulder. "You don't have to. I know exactly what you're talking about."

The sound of a moving truck rattled the nearly empty house.

Ginny snatched at the curtain and swept it aside. "It's them."

Lisa turned and hurried toward the door, calling back as she went, "I hope it all works out for you and Adam, and if it does, be sure to bring a catcher's mitt to the wedding."

"A catcher's mitt? Why?"

"For the bouquet, silly. I'll be aiming it right at you!"

As Ginny watched Lisa fling herself into Billy's open arms, she wished she had the nerve to do the same with Adam.

Instead she stood on the front porch, shifting her weight from one foot to the other as she waited for Adam to get out of the truck and saunter across the small, neatly cropped lawn.

Adam came to the foot of the porch steps and stopped. He said nothing, just stood with his hands tucked into his pockets. Everything from his posture to his expression told her that the next move was hers.

Ginny drew in the sweet smell of freshly mowed grass and the hint of Adam's aftershave. After spending three days with him again and then three days missing him, she felt ready to make that move. She opened her arms and stepped forward, all her senses focused on her happiness and the hope that Adam would reciprocate her emotions.

It would have been a lovely gesture, one of those memorable, tell-the-grandkids-about-it moments. *Would* have been. If Ginny had paid a little less attention to Adam's reaction and a little more to her feet.

She stepped down, but instead of meeting the stairs, her foot just kept going down.

Adam rushed forward.

The heel of her foot pounded to the edge of the second step from the porch, jarring her to her teeth. She reached for the banister.

Adam reached for her.

Just when she thought she had saved herself from falling, Adam's hand on her arm twisted her just enough to slide her heel from the step.

It only took seconds, but it seemed to play out in agonizing slow motion.

Ginny lunged forward.

Adam half chuckled, half barked, "Whoa!"

Her nose met his hard chest.

His chin bounced off the top of her head.

He staggered backward.

She put out her hands to brace herself, which actually only pushed Adam farther off balance.

She heard him groan just seconds before she heard his body make contact with the sidewalk.

Then she fell on top of him, scraping one knee on the rough concrete as she did.

It took her a few stunned seconds to gather the strength to take a deep breath and push up onto her knees.

When she pulled away, Adam propped himself up on his elbows and looked at her, his hat knocked as lopsided as his grin. "Well, I've heard of falling for someone, but until now I've never actually experienced the phenomenon."

"What can I say?" She rubbed her smarting palm over her jeans. "Looks like when it comes to me, Buckman, you're just a regular pushover."

"You always did knock me off my feet, Gin." He sat up, bringing his face just inches from hers. Her eyes glittered with sincerity and longing as he took her injured hand in his, brushed it gently, and asked, "The question is, what are we going to do about it?"

She thought about Lisa's offer to toss her the bouquet, about Adam's apology note that showed her that he valued her feelings, and about his boast that he would sweep her off her feet so she'd want to be his wife.

A small flutter started in Ginny's belly, then worked its way up to put a tremor in her voice. "I guess we get up and get on with the rest of our lives."

His brow tightened.

"Together," she added.

His face lit up. He leaned forward to give her a quick kiss.

No sooner had his lips met hers than Lisa and Billy approached them.

"Wow," Billy said. "Are you two hurt?"

"Yeah," Adam murmured, lifting his mouth from hers just long enough to make himself understood. "Ginny is, and I'm kissing it to make it all better."

Billy hooted. "That'd make sense if she fell on her face, Buckman."

Busted, Adam drew away, his eyes sparkling. He picked up Ginny's hand and placed one tender kiss on her chafed palm.

A shiver tingled down her spine.

"I guess this means you two are okay?" Lisa asked.

Without taking his gaze from Ginny's, Adam nodded. "We're just fine. In fact, we're better than fine. Wouldn't you say, Gin?"

"Much, much better," she whispered to him, her heart filling with the hope that they had come so far and now could start thinking about the future and all it held for them.

Maybe a June wedding, she thought as Adam helped her stand up. *Or July.* Now that they both wanted the same things from their relationship, why rush? She'd have to finish out the school year and make so many plans for moving and finding another job near Tulsa.

She took Adam's arm and gave it a squeeze. Now that she knew he truly respected her feelings and would listen to her side of things before making any decisions, Ginny felt she had all the time in the world.

Adam couldn't take his eyes off Ginny. All afternoon he'd found excuses to linger in the same room she was working in. Watching her perform the simple tasks that helped Lisa turn the house into a home played on his male pride as he imagined her transforming his own sparsely furnished place into *their* home.

"What do you think?" She cocked her head, sending her ponytail swinging, as she took a step away from the golden oval frame she'd just hung.

"Perfect," he murmured, his gaze pointedly on Ginny.

"The mirror, cowboy." She jerked her thumb over her shoulder. "Is it the right height?"

"How would *I* know?"

"Well, can you see yourself?"

He moved in on her in swift silence. When he had his arms wound around her small waist, he pulled her close and bent his head to look deep into her eyes. "Yes, I can. I can see myself doing this exact kind of thing with you."

"*This* kind of thing?" She looped her arms around his neck and stole a peck on the cheek.

"Yeah, that." He smiled, tightening his grip to bring her closer still. "And all this domestic type stuff, too. Hanging your favorite pictures over my fireplace, your college degrees next to mine in the den. So what about you? Can you see yourself doing that, too?"

"Ginny? I need the hammer," Lisa called from another room.

"Gotta go," Ginny whispered, pushing away from his chest.

Adam snagged her back to him, refusing to let her leave just yet. "You haven't answered my question, Gin. Can you see yourself making your home with me? As soon as we're married, of course?"

"Yes, I can." She gave him a fleeting kiss, then slipped from his arms.

"Good," he told her as she picked up the hammer and scooted out the door.

"What's good?" Billy strolled in just then.

"God is good, my friend." Adam tossed his arm over his friend's shoulders.

"Have to agree with you there."

"While you're being agreeable, then, how about you let me borrow the moving truck now that you're done with it?"

"Sure, but what for?"

"I'm cooking up a little surprise for Ginny."

"And you need a fourteen-foot truck for it? You're scaring me, buddy."

Adam slapped his friend on the back. "I just want the truck to move her belongings to my house."

"Uh, Adam, that doesn't exactly sound like the kind of thing you want to do as a surprise." Billy shook his head.

Adam laughed off his friend's concern. "She just told me it's what she wants, Billy. How much of a surprise can it be?"

SEVEN

"Y ou want to what?" Ginny gritted her teeth, feeling her face grow hot.

"Load up your stuff to take to my house." Adam tipped his hat to the back of his head. He shifted his big boots on her porch step and folded his arms across his chest. "I know it's rushing things a little, but we have all day free until the wedding rehearsal and dinner tonight, so why not make good use of it and the truck?"

"The truck?" She felt her head shake but could not honestly say she'd meant to move it. She felt too stunned to connect to anything, even Adam's words.

"Yeah, the truck." He glanced over his shoulder at his pickup parked in her driveway, then added, "Not *my* truck. The one Billy rented. We can go over and get it anytime we want. He doesn't have to have it back until five o'clock today."

She blinked; then a flood of relief washed over her. She laughed aloud. "Oh, Adam, you really had me going."

"What?"

She threw both hands up and said, "April Fools!"

"April what?"

"April Fools!" She forced a laugh. "I get it. You can stop the charade now."

He scowled.

"It *is* a charade, Adam." It had to be. "You couldn't possibly have come over here thinking you would load up my furniture to haul it off to your house *today.*"

"But you said you wanted…" Adam paused. "Ginny, did you or did you not say yesterday that you wanted us to get married and set up our own home?"

"Well, yes." Her hands gripped her hips, the soft fabric of her flowing print dress crinkling under the pads of her fingertips. "But I didn't mean today!"

"Why not?"

Why not? She still wanted to believe he would break into a big grin and yell "April Fools!" any minute. When he didn't, she groaned. "It's happening too fast, that's why not, Adam."

"Too fast? We only dated for three years, more than half of which you spent wanting us to get married."

He had her there. If he'd have shown up with this very same truck a day, a week, even one month after their breakup, she'd have run him over trying to get her things loaded in before he changed his mind again. Suddenly she remembered the source of her hesitation.

Adam reached out to take her by the shoulders. "Look, Gin, I told you when I showed up in your class that I expected you to agree to be my wife before the end of the week. You did and—hey, is that what's bugging you? That I didn't make a formal proposal?"

"No, Adam."

"It is!" He bent at the knees to level his gaze with hers. "I can tell it is."

"If you really think that, Adam, if you haven't learned any more about what I want, what I need, from a husband than that, then—"

"Ginny, I read the verse you suggested. I am making every effort to be more considerate like it says and to show how ready I am to commit to this, just like you wanted when we

235

broke up six months ago." His hands dropped from her shoulders. The morning sun glinted off his truck. "That's why I arranged to use the truck, to show you, not just tell you, how much I want you in my life. And to be considerate and take care of your needs without having to be asked."

"Oh, Adam." Part of her wanted to pull him into an embrace and laugh over the miscommunication. But she just couldn't do it, not with something this important at stake. "I do appreciate the effort, but don't you see?"

He set his jaw and stared straight at her.

"Your doing this, making these plans without even talking to me about them, is just the flip side of the same old coin, Adam." A flash of pain strangled her voice and made her catch her breath as the truth of what she was saying sank into her own heart. "It's all about you, isn't it? First our relationship was guided by your timetable and now…"

Warm tears washed her vision, but she angled her chin up to keep them from falling. She would not allow this moment to be reduced to a crying jag. "This shows me that nothing has really changed. You still don't really have respect for my feelings in our relationship."

She turned on her heel, needing desperately to get away.

Adam snatched at her arm. "Ginny, I don't understand. That is, I understand that you don't want to move your belongings right now, but I *don't* understand what you're saying about us."

"Us?" She peeled his fingers from her arm. "There is no 'us.' I was a fool to think that there ever could be."

She went inside, trying to slam the door, but Adam caught the closing door in one hand.

"I have nothing more to say to you, Adam."

"Good. Then maybe you can listen for a change."

She started to protest, but he spoke before she could.

"I've tried, Ginny. Sure, maybe my attempts have been clumsy and off track, but they've been sincere. I wonder if you can say the same about yours."

"My what?"

"I read the verse you suggested, Gin. And I can't get that Aretha Franklin song 'Respect' out of my head," he said. "When I saw the subtle changes in you, I took that to mean we were both trying."

"Changes? In me?" She flicked her loose hair from her shoulder and crossed her arms over the soft bodice of her dress. "What changes?"

He opened his mouth to speak, then shut it. He glared at her a moment. Finally he tore his gaze away, focusing on something in the sunlit distance.

"Oh." He shifted his lean hips. "Now I get it. It was all one-sided all along. Wasn't it, Ginny?"

"Get what? *What* was all one-sided all along?" She stepped forward. "Adam, I have no idea what you're talking about."

"It's not what *I'm* talking about but what *you* were talking about that's the problem here, Ginny."

She looked at him, perplexed.

"Your lecture." His gaze met hers dead-on. "The demands of me, the verse you suggested, even that song. You didn't share any of them in a spirit of compromise, did you?"

"Well, yes, that is, I intended—"

"Your intentions shine through pretty clearly, Ginny. You intended that I do all the changing and make all the sacrifices in order to keep this relationship alive. You dished out the very same thing you accused me of doing six months ago."

She blinked, unable to process this accusation even as some part of her grasped the truth of his words.

"I admit," he continued, "I am guilty as charged. But when I came to terms with my selfishness and knew that our love, what we had, was worth changing for, I made the effort."

"Oh, Adam, I didn't mean to—" She put her fingertips to her throbbing temple. "I—I need a few minutes to sort all this through."

"I'll be in town until tomorrow after the wedding." He turned on his heel. "If I don't hear from you by then, well, I hope God gives you what you're looking for."

She rushed to the threshold, and the door fell against her shoulder.

"Adam, please!" But he climbed into his truck and revved the engine. As she watched him drive away, she realized she had spent far too much time dwelling on Adam's part of the relationship and not enough dwelling on hers. And if she ever hoped to redeem that relationship, she'd better get to work rectifying that immediately.

Fortunately, she knew just where to start.

Your beauty should not come from outward adornment, such as braided hair and the wearing of gold jewelry and fine clothes. Instead, it should be that of your inner self, the unfading beauty of a gentle and quiet spirit, which is of great worth in God's sight. For this is the way the holy women of the past who put their hope in God used to make themselves beautiful. They were submissive to their own husbands....

"Submissive," Ginny murmured as she lifted her gaze from 1 Peter. That word had always been a sticking point for Ginny. It was probably the very reason she'd concentrated more on the instructions given to men than on those given to women. Ginny cradled the Bible to her chest for a moment. If men behaved as they should, using consideration and respect for women, she thought, maybe the idea of trusting, of giving over to a more gentle nature might not be so...so... frightening.

But then, she thought, this wasn't some abstract study in the behavior between men and women she was dealing with. This was Adam.

Adam *had* changed, *had* become the kind of man the verses admonished him to be. Or at least he had tried. She understood now that as she had unwittingly softened her appearance and her behavior toward Adam these last few days, Adam had responded, just as the verses said he would.

Now the man she loved and her own faith called on her to do more.

She went back to the third chapter of 1 Peter, where she had left off at verse 6, the reference to Sarah. Smiling, she knew what she must do as she read aloud, "You are her daughters if you do what is right and do not give way to fear."

It all became clear to Ginny. If she did the right thing and did not give in to her fear, she and Adam might still make a life together. That is, if he hadn't given up on her completely.

EIGHT

A gush of cool air swept over Ginny as she pushed open the doors of Faith Lutheran Church. She turned on her heel to the right and tried not to let her shoes click too loudly on the hard floor before she reached the carpeted entryway outside the sanctuary.

The main double doors were shut, but one of the side doors stood propped open. Ginny peeked inside. There was a reverent hush in the room. Lisa, her two attendants, and her mother sat whispering in the front pew. Adam, Billy, the pastor, and the other groomsmen huddled a few feet away in front of the altar.

What now? Ginny thought. She'd seen movies where someone had burst into a wedding scene just as the minister asked if anyone knew why the couple could not marry. It hardly fit this situation, though she wished she had some equally dramatic and convenient opportunity to announce both her presence and her motivations for showing up.

She hesitated, lingering at the back of the sanctuary with her hand on the piano. The minister looked up and straight at her.

"Oh, good, your accompanist is here," the pastor said.

"Me?" Ginny clutched at her neckline. "I—I'm not—"

"Ginny!" Adam stepped forward, annoyance in his tone and expression. "What are you doing here?"

She shouldn't have come. Adam wasn't glad to see her. The

realization brought tears to her eyes and a knot to her stomach. "I came to—that is, I hoped—"

What had she hoped? That he'd break into a huge smile and come running down the aisle to take her into his arms and make a loving reconciliation? She thought of her own overused motto, Fool me once, shame on you, but fool me twice, shame on me, and wondered if there was a third option: Fool me three times, it's a shame I can't melt into the floorboards and ooze out of here.

She wanted to leave, to do anything but come face-to-face with Adam and his still-fresh anger. Ignoring the ache in her heart and the burning in her cheeks, Ginny tossed her head back and said, "Maybe I shouldn't have come here at all."

Adam set his jaw and did not reply.

Ginny swallowed hard and took a step back.

"Oh, no, no." Lisa stood and rushed into the aisle at the front of the church. "I'm glad you came, Ginny. I can really use your help."

"You can?" Ginny, Adam, and Billy spoke simultaneously.

"For what?" Adam then demanded.

"A stand-in bride," Lisa said.

"A *what?*" Ginny, not too obviously, leaned on the piano for support.

"A stand-in for me, you know, so I can see how it's going to look." When Ginny looked skeptical, Lisa continued. "Besides, it's bad luck for the bride and groom to stand at the altar together before the actual ceremony. Not that I'm superstitious, mind you, but, well, what do you say, Ginny? Will you help me out?"

What an awkward situation. But what could Ginny do? It was either give in to Lisa's request and put up a gracious front or go back to trying to explain why she'd just shown up uninvited to try to reach a man who seemed to have no interest in her anymore.

"Um, sure, Lisa, I'll do whatever I can to help," Ginny finally murmured. She felt Adam's gaze on her face but decided she must avoid eye contact with him at all costs.

"All right, then." The pastor clapped his hands.

Ginny flinched.

"If you'll just come down here, young lady, we might as well go over that part of the ceremony while we wait for the pianist to arrive."

"Okay." Ginny started down the side aisle.

"Wait, Ginny, come this way." Lisa made a broad gesture to indicate she should come down the center aisle.

Ginny froze.

"I want to see if these candle holders block out the attendants when they come down the aisle." Lisa put her hand on the brass fixtures attached to the two front rows. Her request made sense. Not good sense. But it was not the kind of thing Ginny felt prepared to argue over in front of the wedding party in general and Adam in particular.

She scooted around the piano and over to the center aisle. Despite the fact that she took long, confident strides in silence instead of the slow, timed-to-grand-music pace, Ginny couldn't help feeling like a real bride heading toward her groom. It didn't help matters that every time she glanced up, she found Adam's intent gaze on her.

The irony of it all might have made her laugh out loud if not for the profound sense that her own foolish pride had cost her the trust and respect of a good man.

By the time she reached the front of the church, a flurry of activity had already begun. The attendants hurried forward, the groomsmen, likewise, and Lisa gave a crisp nod and a thumbs-up. Ginny supposed that affirmation meant either the candlesticks were fine or perhaps Lisa felt they'd fooled everyone with this last-ditch cover-up.

"Now, young lady, if you'll stand here." The pastor pointed to a spot directly in front of him. "Bridesmaids here, and groomsmen over there." He waved his hands like an orchestra leader directing a symphony, and everyone obeyed.

"There." He held his hands palms down to signal all was settled. "Now, let's go over the vows."

"Excuse me, Pastor." Lisa stood, her arms folded and her head tipped to one side. "I hate to interrupt, but if I could talk to Billy for just one second…"

"You're not going to back out, are you?" The grin stretched over Billy's face indicated he didn't suspect any such thing.

"Just come here and don't argue," Lisa said with feigned agitation.

Billy rolled his eyes and sighed. "Already she's giving orders."

"And already you're following them," Adam said.

Billy paid the comment the due it deserved by turning his back on his friend and going to Lisa. The couple put their heads together to whisper for a moment; then Lisa looked up. "Pastor, since we're going to have these candles up front, can we see how it will look with them lit and the overhead lights dimmed just a tiny bit?"

"Certainly, my dear. Let me see if I can find the switches." He hurried off, muttering to himself.

"Patrick, why don't you help Pastor?" Billy called out to his younger brother, the other groomsman.

The young man made himself scarce in an instant, and Ginny realized that Lisa had motioned away the bridesmaids.

Ginny and Adam had been left alone at the church's altar.

"Imagine meeting you here." It sounded harder than Adam intended, but he couldn't really help it. She'd caught him off guard just appearing at the church like this. Not that she hadn't been on his mind constantly since he'd left her this morning, but for her to come here now, well, he just wasn't sure how to handle it. He would not be made a fool of again, that much he did know.

But when his eyes met hers, his resolve went out the stained-glass window. He studied her in the warm, glowing light of the sanctuary.

She bowed her head, but before she did he saw regret and pain flash over her face.

His heart leapt in an erratic rhythm. She loved him. He knew it. And he loved her. Maybe neither of them knew how to love perfectly or exactly as the other had always dreamed of being loved. But they loved each other all the same. And he knew now that they were both willing to sacrifice to make that love work.

He watched her stand beside him before the altar with its gleaming cross, the reminder of the greatest love of all. He prayed that she would see that if they both gave in just a little and worked together, they could have a wonderful marriage.

Adam cleared his throat, then jerked his head in the direction in which the wedding party had last been seen slipping quietly away. "They aren't exactly subtle, are they?"

"Says the man who burst into my classroom and threw me over his shoulder." Only the hint of a smile softened her wary expression.

"I am really, truly, absolutely sorry for that, Gin."

She held up one hand. "You've already made your apologies for that, Adam. Now it's my turn."

"Your turn?" *If they both gave in just a little…*

She nodded.

"To apologize?" He wondered if that sounded as eager as he felt.

"Yes."

"For what?"

"Let's see. For being bossy and demanding." She held her fingers up to tick off the reasons, her eyes fixed on his. "Inconsiderate, selfish, narrow-minded…Aren't you going to jump in and stop me at some point here?"

"What? And have you accuse me of not respecting your opinion?" He grinned, though still testing her.

"Okay, I guess I deserved that." She glanced away. "And you deserve an apology. I was wrong to place all our problems on your shoulders. Relationships need work from both partners."

Adam took her hand in his. "When you say 'relationships,' do you mean marriage?"

Ginny lifted her gaze to meet his as she whispered, "I do."

The simple words rattled through him. He gripped her hand tighter. "Tell me that the next time you stand at an altar and say those words, we'll be taking marriage vows."

"Yes." She barely made a sound. Her beautiful eyes widened, awash with unshed tears.

He leaned down to give her a kiss, but before his lips met hers, she sniffed and added, "On one condition."

"Condition?" His cheek twitched.

"When it's time to carry me across the threshold, promise me you won't sling me over your shoulder."

He fit his hand to the small of her back. "That's your only condition?"

"Well…" Her gaze dipped to his mouth. "If anything else should come up, I'm sure we can work it out together."

He kissed her fully, pulling her tightly to him as if he feared she might get away again. Only the sound of giggles and finally a hearty hoot from Billy jarred Adam and Ginny out of their very sweet celebration.

Keeping her in his arms, Adam put his forehead to Ginny's and said, "Is it just me or do you feel like we've been set up?"

"Well, it *is* April Fools' Day." She wound her arms around his waist. "But I sure don't feel like a fool, do you?"

"Uh-huh."

"You do?" She blinked in surprise.

"Yep. A fool for you."

"Then that's one thing we have in common."

"Really? You're actually saying a man and a woman can have the same reaction to their loved one?" he teased.

"Man *or* woman, Adam. With the right attitude, the right person, and God's guidance, we can make it all work out."

Happily ignoring the hoots and applause of the bridal party around them, he kissed her again.

THE PALISADES LINE

Look for these new releases at your local bookstore. If the title you seek is not in stock, the store may order you a copy using the ISBN listed.

Heartland Skies, Melody Carlson
ISBN 1-57673-264-9

Jayne Morgan moves to the small town of Paradise with the prospect of marriage, a new job, and plenty of horses to ride. But when her fiancé dumps her, she's left with loose ends. Then she wins a horse in a raffle, and the handsome rancher who boards her horse makes things look decidedly better.

Memories, Peggy Darty (May 1998)
ISBN 1-57673-171-5

In this sequel to *Promises*, Elizabeth Calloway is left with amnesia after witnessing a hit-and-run accident. Her husband, Michael, takes her on a vacation to Cancún so that she can relax and recover her memory. What they don't realize is that the killer is following them, hoping to wipe out Elizabeth's memory permanently....

Remembering the Roses, Marion Duckworth (June 1998)
ISBN 1-57673-236-3

Sammie Sternberg is trying to escape her memories of the man who betrayed her, and she ends up in a small town on the Olympic Peninsula in Washington. There she opens her dream business—an antique shop in an old Victorian—and meets a reclusive watercolor artist who helps to heal her broken heart.

Waterfalls, Robin Jones Gunn
ISBN 1-57673-221-5

In a visit to Glenbrooke, Oregon, Meredith Graham meets movie star Jacob Wilde and is sure he's the one. But when Meri puts her foot in her mouth, things fall apart. Is isn't until the two of them get thrown together working on a book-and-movie project that Jacob realizes his true feelings, and this time he's the one who's starstruck.

China Doll, Barbara Jean Hicks (June 1998)
ISBN 1-57673-262-2
Bronson Bailey is having a mid-life crisis: after years of globetrotting in his journalism career, he's feeling restless. Georgine Nichols has also reached a turning point: after years of longing for a child, she's decided to adopt. The problem is, now she's fallen in love with Bronson, and he doesn't want a child.

Angel in the Senate, Kristen Johnson Ingram (April 1998)
ISBN 1-57673-263-0
Newly elected senator Megan Likely heads to Washington with high hopes for making a difference in government. But accusations of election fraud, two shocking murders, and threats on her life make the Senate take a backseat. She needs to find answers, but she's not sure whom she can trust anymore.

Irish Rogue, Annie Jones
ISBN 1-57673-189-8
Michael Shaughnessy has paid the price for stealing a pot of gold, and now he's ready to make amends to the people he's hurt. Fiona O'Dea is number one on his list. The problem is, Fiona doesn't want to let Michael near enough to hurt her again. But before she knows it, he's taken his Irish charm and worked his way back into her life…and her heart.

Forgotten, Lorena McCourtney
ISBN 1-57673-222-3
A woman wakes up in an Oregon hospital with no memory of who she is. When she's identified as Kat Cavanaugh, she returns to her home in California. As Kat struggles to recover her memory,

she meets a fiancé she doesn't trust and an attractive neighbor who can't believe how she's changed. She begins to wonder if she's really Kat Cavanaugh, but if she isn't, what happened to the real Kat?

The Key, Gayle Roper (April 1998)
ISBN 1-57673-223-1
On Kristie Matthews's first day living on an Amish farm, she gets bitten by a dog and is rushed to the emergency room by a handsome stranger. In the ER, an elderly man in the throes of a heart attack hands her a key and tells her to keep it safe. Suddenly odd accidents begin to happen to her, but no one's giving her any answers.

— ANTHOLOGIES —

Fools for Love, Ball, Brooks, Jones
ISBN 1-57673-235-5
By Karen Ball: Kitty starts pet-sitting, but when her clients turn out to be more than she can handle, she enlists help from a handsome handyman.
By Jennifer Brooks: Caleb Murphy tries to acquire a book collection from a widow, but she has one condition: he must marry her granddaughter first.
By Annie Jones: A college professor who has been burned by love vows not to be fooled twice, until her ex-fiancé shows up and ruins her plans!

Heart's Delight, Ball, Hicks, Noble
ISBN 1-57673-220-7
By Karen Ball: Corie receives a Valentine's Day date from her sisters and thinks she's finally found the one…until she learns she went out with the wrong man.

By Barbara Jean Hicks: Carina and Reid are determined to break up their parents' romance, but when it looks like things are working, they have a change of heart.

By Diane Noble: Two elderly bird-watchers set aside their differences to try to save a park from disaster but learn they've bitten off more than they can chew.

Sunsets, **Robin Jones Gunn** (ISBN 1-57673-103-0)
Alissa Benson has a run-in at work with Brad Phillips, and is more than a little upset when she finds out he's her neighbor!

Snow Swan, **Barbara Jean Hicks** (ISBN 1-57673-107-3)
Toni, an unwed mother and a recovering alcoholic, falls in love for the first time. But if Clark finds out the truth about her past, will he still love her?

Irish Eyes, **Annie Jones** (ISBN 1-57673-108-1)
Julia Reed gets drawn into a crime involving a pot of gold and has her life turned upside down by Interpol agent Cameron O'Dea.

Father by Faith, **Annie Jones** (ISBN 1-57673-117-0)
Nina Jackson buys a dude ranch and hires cowboy Clint Cooper as her foreman, but her son, Alex, thinks Clint is his new daddy!

Stardust, **Shari MacDonald** (ISBN 1-57673-109-X)
Gillian Spencer gets her dream assignment but is shocked to learn she must work with Maxwell Bishop, who once broke her heart.

Kingdom Come, **Amanda MacLean** (ISBN 1-57673-120-0)
Ivy Rose Clayborne, M.D., pairs up with the grandson of the coal baron to fight the mining company that is ravaging her town.

Dear Silver, **Lorena McCourtney** (ISBN 1-57673-110-3)
When Silver Sinclair receives a letter from Chris Bentley ending their relationship, she's shocked, since she's never met the man!

Enough! **Gayle Roper** (ISBN 1-57673-185-5)
When Molly Gregory gets fed up with her three teenaged children, she announces that she's going on strike.

A Mother's Love, **Bergren, Colson, MacLean**
(ISBN 1-57673-106-5)
Three heartwarming stories share the joy of a mother's love.

Silver Bells, **Bergren, Krause, MacDonald**
(ISBN 1-57673-119-7)
Three novellas focus on romance during Christmastime.